Full Cicada Moon

Marilyn Hilton

DIAL BOOKS FOR YOUNG READERS

an imprint of Penguin Group (USA) LLC

DIAL BOOKS FOR YOUNG READERS
Published by the Penguin Group
Penguin Group (USA) LLC
375 Hudson Street
New York, New York 10014

USA/Canada/UK/Ireland/Australia/New Zealand/India/South Africa/China

penguin.com

A Penguin Random House Company

Library of Congress Cataloging-in-Publication Data

Hilton, Marilyn.
Full cicada moon / by Marilyn Hilton.   pages cm
Summary: In 1969 twelve-year-old Mimi and her family move to an all-white town
in Vermont, where Mimi's mixed-race background and interest in "boyish" topics like
astronomy make her feel like an outsider.
ISBN 978-0-525-42875-6 (hardcover)
[1. Novels in verse. 2. Racially mixed people]—Fiction. 3. Sex role]—Fiction.] I. Title.

PZ7.5.H56Fu 2015   [Fic]—dc23   2014044894

Printed in the United States of America

1 3 5 7 9 10 8 6 4 2

Designed by Mina Chung • Text set in Perpetua

For

Keiko and Robert, Lois and James Wesley,

and their families

Be loving enough

to absorb evil

and understanding enough

to turn an enemy into a friend.

—Dr. Martin Luther King Jr.

「ひとりの人間にとっては小さな一歩だが、

人類にとっては偉大な飛躍である。」

"That's one small step for [a] man,

one giant leap for mankind."

—Neil Armstrong

Full Cicada Moon

Flying to Vermont—January 1, 1969

I wish we had flown to Vermont
instead of riding
on a bus, train, train, bus
all the way from Berkeley.
Ten hours would have soared, compared to six days.
But two plane tickets—
one for me and one for Mama—
would have cost a lot of money,
and Papa already spent so much
when he flew home at Thanksgiving.

Mama is sewing buttons on my new slacks
and helping me fill out the forms
for my new school in Hillsborough, our new town.
This might be a new year
but seventh grade is halfway done,
and I'll be the new girl.

I'm stuck at the Ethnicity part.

Check only one, it says.

The choices are:

> White
>
> Black
>
> Puerto Rican
>
> Portuguese
>
> Hispanic
>
> Oriental
>
> Other

I am

half Mama,

half Papa,

and all me.

Isn't that all anyone needs to know?

But the form says *All items must be completed,*

so I ask, "Other?"

Mama pushes her brows together,

making what Papa calls her Toshirō-Mifune face.

"Check all that apply," she says.

"But it says just one."

"Do you listen to your mother or a piece of paper?"

I check off Black,
cross out Oriental,
and write *Japanese* with a check mark.

"What will we do now, Mimi-chan?" Mama asks,
which means: Will you read
or do algebra, so you're not behind?
"Take a nap," I say.

Mama frowns,
but I close my eyes
and pretend we're flying.
The bus driver is the pilot
and every bump in the road
becomes an air pocket in the sky.

Hatsuyume

A jolt wakes me up. I was dreaming
my *hatsuyume*—the first dream of the new year.
If I tell my *hatsuyume*, it won't come true
because in Japanese, *speak* sounds just like *let go*.
And if my dream meant good luck, I don't want to
let it go.

I dreamed I was a bird, strong and brown
and fast
with feathers tipped magenta and gold.
I shot straight up into the air like a Saturn rocket,
then swooped and dove, the sun warming my back.
I pumped my wings, then glided
over the desert
and the sea.

The air filled my lungs,
the wind lifted my wings
higher and higher
over the mountains
and above the clouds.
The moon grew large,
and I stretched to touch it.

Maybe it was a good-luck dream
and this will be a good year
for Papa and Mama and me.
That's what I hope.

But, what if my *hatsuyume* meant bad luck?
Mama says to let go of your bad dreams by telling
them.
Papa says to bury your bad dreams
in a hole as deep as your elbow.
The ground in New England is frozen,
so if I listen to Papa, I'll have to wait until spring.
I'll listen to Mama instead
and write my dream on paper,
so either way—good luck or bad—
my *hatsuyume* will not be spoken.

I have never flown before
but one day

                                               soar.

                        will

            I

Waxing Gibbous

I study

The Old Farmer's Almanac
that Santa had put in my stocking
from cover to cover.

I like

reading about the moon,
and I've memorized
all its names and phases.

I know

the moon tonight
is waxing gibbous, almost
the Full Wolf Moon.
It has chased us outside the bus window
all the way from Boston,

bounding through the sky,
skipping across rooftops,
dodging trees
like it has one   last   word
to tell us.

                              I remember
Papa said
if you leave eggs under a waxing moon,
all your chicks will hatch.

And Mama said
if you make a wish on the moon
over your shoulder,
it will come true.

                              I whisper
to the moon on my shoulder:

                              "I wish
all my dreams will hatch."

Reflections

This bus lulls.
Some people are reading, some are sleeping,
two ladies behind us are talking,
the baby up front chuckles hoarsely,
someone is sipping tomato soup,
and in back, Glen Campbell is singing "Wichita
Lineman" on the radio.
All of us who don't know one another
are riding together on this Trailways bus to Vermont
on the first night of 1969.

It doesn't feel like *oshōgatsu*, New Year's Day,
because Mama couldn't make *ozōni* and sushi
and black-eyed peas and collard greens,
and we couldn't sip warm sake from the shallow
cups.

Mama says she doesn't care about those things
because we're traveling to meet Papa.
But what bothers her
is that no man crossed our threshold this morning
(because we don't have a threshold today),
and that means we'll have bad luck all year.
I told her we can find a man to visit our new
house,
but she said, "Too late."

The lady across the aisle is knitting a scarf.
She has been staring at Mama and me
ever since the sun set.
I want to stick out my tongue at her reflection in our
window
just to let her know
I know,
but that would disgrace Mama
and disappoint Papa.

So, I open the *Time* magazine
with the three Apollo 8 astronauts on the cover—
the Men of the Year—
that came just before we left,

which Auntie Sachi slipped into my bag at the door,

with a note:

いってらっしゃい

Have a safe journey.

Arriving

I can tell by the way Mama looks at herself
in the window, brushes her bangs to the side,
and runs her finger under her eyes
that we'll be in Hillsborough soon,
where Papa, in the tweed coat he calls "professorial,"
will meet us.
She pops a wintergreen Life Savers in her mouth
and passes the roll to me.
I take one
because I want my kiss on Papa's cheek to be fresh.

The bus slows down.
A barbershop, an insurance company,
a dentist's office, a grocery store
all slide by. The air prickles

and everyone sits up straight and shifts in their seats,
finishes talking to the person next to them.
"Hillsborough coming up!" the driver calls.

The lady across the aisle winds up her yarn
and tucks her knitting into a tote bag. She looks at
me again
and leans into the aisle. "Are you adopted?"
"*Nani?*" Mama asks me. She must have been
daydreaming
or she would have asked, "What?"
I whisper, "She wants to know where we're going."
Mama glances at the lady and turns into Mifune.

But before she can pretend she doesn't speak English,
I say, "She's my mom."
The lady looks at me, then at Mama,
and shakes her head.
"No . . . she's not your mother."

The bus pulls up in front of a diner
and stops so quick
that we all jerk forward in our seats.
The driver cranks a handle and

the door hisses open.
He disappears outside
as cold air scampers down the aisle.

Papa is waiting in front of the diner
wearing his coat
and a red-and-gold scarf, Hillsborough College
colors.
When he sees me inside the bus, he waves.
But I wave harder.

Outside, I hold his hand in his pocket
while he counts our suitcases—four plus my
overnight case.
The icy air pinches my cheeks,
but my heart is warm.
He drapes his scarf around my throat
and says, "Now you're the professor."

The knitting lady steps down from the bus
for a breath of air.
"And this is my dad. See?" I say, and smile.
She looks at Papa, at Mama,
and back at me. Then,

not smiling, she says, "Yes, I see,"
and walks toward the diner.

When I know Mama and Papa can't see me,
I stick out my tongue
so far that it hurts.

New House

Our new house smells like varnish and
balsam needles and mothballs.
The floors are all wood, except the kitchen and the
bathrooms,
which are linoleum,
and they creak when I walk around in my socks—
which I can't do for long
because it's so *cold* that my scalp tightens.
Halfway up the stairs is a stained-glass window
with a picture of flowers and butterflies in a garden,
like spring.

Papa opens the cellar door and flips the light switch.
I peer down the dark, dusty staircase.
And in the kitchen sink are the bowl and spoon Papa
used for his cornflakes this morning.

He shows Mama the cinnamon-colored dishwasher
built under the counter
and the garbage disposal built into the sink.
These are firsts for Mama.
She opens the dishwasher door and pulls out the top
rack.
"Hmm," she says, and that's all.
Papa and I look at each other.
We know we'll find out what that means,
but it won't be now.

"This is our room," Papa says,
opening a door down the hall.
A big bed with a yellow comforter sits against a wall.
Papa is renting most of the furniture
because we didn't own much in California.
Before Mama and I left Berkeley,
she shipped her tall china cupboard and her *kotatsu*,
the low table with a heater underneath.

"Where's my room?" I ask.
Papa takes my hand and leads me up a steep staircase.
My room is at the top. It's the biggest bedroom I've
ever seen.

One side of the ceiling slopes halfway to the floor
and seats are built under the two windows.
"If you don't like it, you can trade with us," Papa says.
But I say no—
so fast that he can't take this room away.

Later, Mama comes upstairs to tuck me in,
like I'm five again.
But tonight, because we're in our new house,
in our new town, on the other side of the country,
I want her to.
She sits for a few minutes on my bed,
as if she needs to as much as I
need her to.
Papa has had a week to get used to this new house,
and Mama and I will catch up.
She kisses me good night and tucks the comforter
all the way around my chin
and goes downstairs. The light glows up the stairs,
stretching her shadow on the wall.

The sky outside is soft pink, and I smile into my
comforter.
It is like the soft pink is inside me, resting,

breathing with me.

Is this house making me feel this way,

or the snow outside? Or knowing our long trip is
over?

Or having a big bedroom upstairs

but hearing Mama and Papa downstairs,

and we're a family again after four months?

That's it—

all the good things have come together

in soft pink

happiness.

First Night

This house creaks
like it can't find a comfortable place to settle into.
I toss and turn
and can't find a comfortable spot to sleep in.
My clock says 2:18 a.m.
I get out of bed and sit at a window.

The sky has cleared
and the moon sits high in the sky
like a pearl button.
Stars—bright, cold, voiceless—
are winking, but I know that's because Earth's heat
is rising,
the atmosphere is shifting.
(A future astronaut needs to know these things.)
I wonder if Earth winked at the Apollo 8 astronauts

when they took its picture from the moon on
Christmas Eve.

Something moves in the next yard.
A dog, dark and fuzzy, leaps in the moonlit snow.
Then one sharp whistle from the neighbor's house
calls it inside.

Like Saturday

The sun wakes me up.
Ouch! my neck hurts
because I'm still sitting at my window.
A fringe of icicles hangs outside,
and the sun makes little rainbows inside them.
I smell coffee and bacon,
and I know that hot chocolate is waiting downstairs.

No cornflakes for Papa this morning—
Mama's making her special basted fried eggs with
onions
and the bacon he loves.
Today is Thursday, but it feels like Saturday
because this is still school vacation.
Thursday is the only day that doesn't have a
personality,
so today it borrowed Saturday's.

Mama has already set out her *maneki-neko*,

the cat statue that waves, so we will have good luck

from the start.

It makes our new house feel more like home.

"What's your plan today, Meems?" Papa asks at the

table,

the newspaper open in front of him.

What I really want to do is see that dog again,

but I shrug and say, "Explore."

"It's cold outside," Mama says. "Wear your warm

clothes."

Papa looks up from his paper. "And do not leave the

yard."

Next Door Boy

Wood smoke hangs in a blue haze outside,
and far off
a chain saw buzzes through the air.
An empty coop in our backyard is covered in snow
like a tiny alpine chalet,
but in the spring it will be filled with turkeys.

My lips stick to my teeth
and my nostrils are stuck shut. My chest hurts
when I breathe this icy air.
I'll warm up by making a snowman.
This snow is too deep for rolling three balls for his
body,
so I pack it into a mound,
then sculpt him with my hands.
I pack a lemon-size ball for his nose, poke holes for
his eyes,
and draw a big smile with my thumb.

By the time I'm done,
my skin prickles with sweat under my clothes,
my nose runs,
and my legs shudder.

A boy steps out of the house next door
and kicks snow down the back steps.
The dog from last night bursts past him,
toppling the boy to the snow.
"Pattress!" he calls, laughing.
But she wanders away from him, snuffling
like a steam train.

Even across our wide yards, I can see
the boy's cheeks are red on his pale skin,
slapped by the cold.
Pattress wags her long, pointy tail.
"Hi," I say, raising my hand, sniffling.
The boy raises his hand and nods, then
goes back into the house,
calling, "Come on, Pattress."

The brown dog looks at me, then at the steps,
and follows the boy inside.

Ready for School

These are the new slacks that Mama sewed,
   butterscotch corduroy with three black buttons at
the waist,
   because four would be bad luck.
   This is the sweater that Auntie Phoenix sent from
Baltimore,
   tangerine and fluffy,
   scratching my wrists and neck.
   These are my tights
   and my secondhand boots with a run-down right heel
   that crunch in the snow, leaving waffle footprints.
   This is the wool coat that Mama wore
   the winter she married Papa in Japan.
   And mittens with snowflakes on each palm
   and a long scarf to shield me from the tiny wind
daggers.

When I breathe, my cheeks and chin feel moist
and cold at the same time.
These are my frozen eyelashes
and my Popsicle nose.

You have to wear a lot of clothes
just to go to school in Vermont.

First Day

Papa doesn't want me to take the school bus,
so he's driving me on his way to the college.
When the wind blows the snow, it makes a rainbow.
Rainbows mean hope. I hope for a good day,
good teachers, a good friend.
Deep in my pocket, I touch the round of *omochi*
and a square of corn bread
that Mama wrapped in wax paper
so I can remember our small, late *oshōgatsu*.

I wish we didn't have to live out in the sticks,
but Mama wants to raise turkeys and grow
vegetables,
so even in spring, Papa will take me and bring me
home.

Maybe there's another reason we live two miles from
town
and Papa drives me to school.
Even if we lived in town,
in the kind of house other professors live in—
like that white-shingled Victorian with the black
shutters—
would Papa escort me every morning
and stand guard after the last bell?

Rules

I thought that Papa was going to drop me off
in front of my new junior high.
Instead, he turns into the drive and parks in front
of the PRINCIPAL sign.
Our car is a green Malibu, which Papa drove
all the way from Berkeley to Hillsborough.
One day he'll tell us about that trip
all at once.
Or, maybe he has been telling it all along,
the way snowpack grows:

                                  a million tiny flakes
        drifting
                      one by one,
but I haven't been listening.

"Everything cool?" he asks.
I look out the windshield at the white clapboard
building,

the wide steps up to the front doors,

the tall windows framed in green sashes.

"It's cool," I say, because it's what he wants to hear,

and because so far there's nothing to worry about.

But in my stomach

little ice wings are fluttering.

Then he asks, "Do you want me to go in with you?"

I shrug, which today means yes,

and he knows that. "Just remember," he says,

"be kind, be respectful, and persist."

"Like raindrops on granite," I say,

because we know that's how I persist—

drip, drip, drip

until the granite cracks.

The office smells like warm wood and paper

and sweet mimeograph,

and when the secretary, Miss Holder, gets up from
her desk

and comes to the counter where Papa and I are
standing,

I smell Ambush by Dana perfume.

She has to look up at my tall, dark, handsome dad.

"May I help you?" she asks,

glancing at me, then back to Papa.

"Mimi is starting school today," he says
kindly, and hands her my packet of forms.
That's when she smiles, finally,
and says, "Oh, yes. We've been expecting you."
Maybe she was expecting a new girl from California
but not expecting *me*.

Miss Holder takes a folder from the gray file cabinet,
and taps her pencil as she reads. Then she says
my homeroom teacher will be Mr. Pease and
I'll need to take a test for math.
"Mimi is doing algebra at home," Papa states
respectfully.
"Be that as it may," she says, "the test is required."

"And did she bring a skirt? Girls must wear skirts,"
she says,
as if I'm not standing right here.
"But it's freezing outside," I say.
"It's the dress code. Those are the rules."
Papa gives me a quick hug. "I'll bring you one."
Then I remember he's going to school today, too,
and whisper, "Drip, drip, drip."

Shop

Miss Holder hands me my schedule.
"You travel with the same students to all your classes
except homeroom.
And home ec, of course,
when the boys go to shop class."

"When do the girls go to shop class?" I ask.

Miss Holder frowns,
like my question makes no sense.

Then she says, "They don't.
Girls learn how to cook and sew
so they can be good homemakers.
Why would you want to make a bookcase
when you can make a cake?"

But I want to ask her why wouldn't I.

Getting to Know You

In homeroom, I look for someone
like Marciela, Yu-Lin, Poornima, even creepy Eiji
or the boy from next door.
I don't want to stick out,
don't want to be different
or scared.

Mr. Pease shows me an empty seat in the first row.
My name is written on the chalkboard
and underlined. Mr. Pease smiles, and I like him.
"Stand up, Mimi," he says.
"Do you have a real name?"
"Mimi is my real name."

Then he tells the class they can me ask three
questions.

Michael, with blond hair and braces, goes first.

"Where did you come from?" he asks.

"Berkeley, California." Michael looks puzzled.

"It's near San Francisco," I say, but

he still looks confused.

I look at Mr. Pease,

who nods to a girl with glasses and a brunette flip.

"Vicky."

"What do you want to be when you grow—"

"An astronaut," I answer quickly. I don't have to

think about that.

I look around, expecting nods or smiles,

but everyone laughs. Even Mr. Pease.

"Maybe you should be a comedienne," he says,

and right away I don't like him as much.

"Last question—Carl," he says to a boy reaching his
hand so high

he could pull the tiles out of the ceiling.

"What nationality are you?"

"I'm . . . American."

"I mean . . . what are you?"

And then I understand what Michael had really

been asking.

If everyone was laughing before, they're all quiet now,

as if they all had the same question and made Carl

ask it.

But how do I answer that?

I look at Mr. Pease for help, but his eyes tell me

he has the same question.

It's up to me to solve the puzzle

of how to answer the question

What am I?—

when I know the real question

begins with Who.

Obentō

My mouth waters whenever I think of my lunch
sitting in my new locker
(number 348, combination 36-11-17 . . . or 15?):
hinomaru—one pickled plum on pearl rice—
and grilled salmon,
carrot slices shaped like flowers,
black-eyed peas and collard greens,
and the corn bread.
Mama packed this *obentō* for me, even though
Papa told her a tuna sandwich and a thermos of soup
would be better at this school.

But after what happened in homeroom this morning,
I leave my *obentō* in my locker
and eat the turkey tetrazzini and canned peaches
in the cafeteria
like everyone else.

Hungry

Turkey tetrazzini tastes like a ball of paste,
and these canned peaches
are not like the ones Mama preserved in California.
Whenever she'd open a new jar
in the cold, rainy winter,
it became summer again in my bowl.

Everyone else is talking to everyone else
but not to me. So I eat this food
because I'm starving
and there isn't anything else to do
in this cafeteria
that smells like American cheese and Comet.
Nothing to do but look at my tray and eat
by myself.

Why is that boy over there—
the one in a fifth chair at a table of four—
staring at me?
Mama told me not to be pushy
but wait to be invited.
I smile at the boy. He smiles back
but doesn't invite me to a sixth chair.

Journal

Mr. Pease is also my English teacher.

I'm so glad he doesn't tell me to stand up in this
class

and answer three questions.

"Welcome back from vacation," he says.

His bow tie is crooked, like a propeller ready to spin,

and I imagine him soaring above our heads.

"Did I say something funny, Mimi?" he asks,

and in my mind Mr. Pease drop-lands on his
desk.

I shake my head.

"Stand up, please," he says. "We have fun in my class,

but we work hard

and we don't tolerate clowns."

"Yes, sir," I say, and sit down again.

Feet shuffle on the floor,
and voices around me murmur, "Wooo."

"From now until the end of the year, you'll be
keeping a journal,"
he says, handing out spiral notebooks from a stack
on his desk.
"You'll write, draw, collage, or whatever you want.
But you'll do it at least three times a week."

"Do we have to show them to you?" asks a girl
beside me.
"Do I see a hand, Barbara?" he asks.
Vermont teachers are stricter than teachers in
Berkeley.
Barbara raises her hand. "Do we have to show them
to you?"
"You'll turn them in before the end of the year."

I raise my hand, and Mr. Pease nods.
"What do we write about?"
"Whatever you want."
I raise my hand again, and he says, smiling, "You still
have the floor."

"What kind of writing can we do?"

He leans forward. "Whatever you want, as long as I can read it.

Experiment, try something new."

"Like poetry?" someone asks.

"As long as I can read it."

I know
exactly what I will write in my journal for Mr. Pease,
and by June, he'll understand better
who I am.

Notions

"This spring, you're going to make aprons,"
says Mrs. Olson in home ec.
"And next fall, you'll wear them when you cook."

"Why don't we just *buy* an apron?" someone asks.
I had the same question,
because Mama has plenty of aprons that I can wear
and I'd rather make a skirt.

"Because you're learning how to sew," Mrs. Olson says,
passing out a paper with *Notions* printed at the top
and a picture of the apron—
a rectangle with a pocket and a long strip for the tie.
It looks simple and plain.
If Mama designed this apron, it would be a lot
fancier.

"What are notions?" someone asks.

"They're your thread and your needles and pins.
You can get everything in town."

I have a notion that Mama and I
will go downtown this Saturday.
I have a notion that she'll buy one fabric
with flowers for the bottom part
and another fabric with stripes
for the tie and pocket.
Then she will buy extra fabric for a ruffle
and rickrack for a trim.

And I have notion
that if I sew this apron very fast,
I'll have time to make a skirt.

Science Class

The last class of my first day
is science.
My teacher, Mrs. Stanton, has curly hair
like mine, but hers is light-brown-turning-silver.
She wears a forest green skirt that flares,
a beige turtleneck,
and a cardigan buttoned at the top like a cape.
Her glasses are on a chain.

"It will be May before we know it,"
she says, leaning against her desk,
"and time for the Science Groove."
She waits—for the kids to say something
or clap, but all they do is lean on their arms
or doodle, or yawn and stick out their legs.
They all know what she's talking about. But I don't.

I want to ask what the Groove part is all about.
My arm aches to rise. But,
since I already feel like Mama's *maneki-neko*,
I wait
for someone else to ask.

"I'll help you choose a project," Mrs. Stanton says.
"You'll write a report and do a presentation for ten
minutes.
And, it must be entirely your own work.
No one can do it for you."

Now my hand springs up.
Mrs. Stanton nods. "Wait till I finish,
then you might not have a question anymore.
Everyone will set up their projects in the gym
and the projects will be judged.
The best projects will win awards.
Did that answer your question, Miss Oliver?"
"Yes, thank you."

Here they call it a Groove. In Berkeley
we called it a Fair. I won third prize at the Fair.
At the Groove, I will win first.

Little Lies

After school
Papa is waiting near the buses.
He stands like a giant sequoia,
wearing his tweed coat that Mama made
and his mustache and those glasses—
all he needs is a pipe.
He nods hello
to the kids
who crane their necks to stare
as they pass.
Some ask "Who's that?" and
some glance at me,
guessing the connection.

"How was your first day?" Papa asks,
adjusting my scarf.

I know he wants me to like Hillsborough,
so I shrug and say, "Good."
There was some good, like the Science Groove
and writing in a journal.

"Are we going home now?
Where's the car?"
"I left it at the college," he says. "We'll walk there
so you can see the downtown.
Do you have everything—books
for homework, your lunch box?"
"Yes," I say quickly,
telling the truth about the first part.
I have my books. But my *obentō*
is still in my locker.

Downtown

We head down the street to town—
Papa striding and I with quick, short steps
so I don't slip and crack my head open,
which is Mama's biggest fear.
Everything is white and black and gray
and slush.
Except for the sky, which is . . . sky blue . . . and alive
with sunlight and snow rainbows.

We walk past a lawyer's office, a barbershop,
the Hillsborough Savings Bank, and a drugstore,
where I see toys and a soda fountain
through the frosted window.
Somewhere, a shovel scrapes cement.

We pass—
    A round woman

in a gray coat with big buttons that look like
    mine
and a plaid scarf over her mouth.
She carries a grocery bag
and wipes her eyes with a tissue.

A boy in a blue parka with the hood string pulled
    so tight
his face is a thumb,
and mittens pinned to his cuffs.

A college girl in a long skirt made out of
    jeans
and a short, red sweater.
Her hair bounces around her shoulders as
    she walks.

Each one stares at us until we get close
and then they look away.
Papa says, "Hello,"
and gives a little nod.

Round woman nods back
and clutches her grocery bag.

Boy backs up to a signpost
and twists around it as we pass
to stare.

College girl just keeps on walking,
as if she doesn't see us.
As if she didn't hear
my gentle dad's hello.

Farmer Dell

Our neighbor's house,
where I saw Pattress and the boy,
is long and low, and snuggled into the snow.
There's also a garage that's twice as high as the house.
Old cars and trucks and propane tanks
lie around the yard like lazy farm animals.

A mailbox sits on a post at the end of the driveway,
with DELL stenciled in white letters. Whenever I see it,
I sing "The Farmer in the Dell" in my head.
The man who lives there doesn't look like a farmer,
and I never see a wife or a cow, but I call him
Farmer Dell.

Farmer Dell always wears the same thing—
green work pants, a plaid wool jacket buttoned to
his neck,

and work boots. If it's really cold, he wears a red-
checkered hat
with the flaps over his ears.
Pattress is always with him,
and sometimes when Papa and I drive to school,
she's sitting at the garage door.
But I haven't seen that boy again.

Sometimes Farmer Dell is driving a backhoe,
clearing snow in the yard. In the afternoon
another car or truck will be lying in the nest he made.
Sometimes he's walking to his mailbox
or standing beside it.
And sometimes he's pushing a snowblower
down his driveway.
The snow cascades into a perfect trim,
like piping on a birthday cake.

Every time we pass by our neighbor,
Papa waves to him.
But no matter what Farmer Dell is doing,
he never waves back.
Each time he doesn't wave back,
my mouth goes dry.

This morning, I ask, "Why?"

Papa says, "Maybe he can't see very well.

Or maybe he doesn't like us."

That is why my mouth goes dry.

"But he doesn't even know us."

Papa shifts his hands on the steering wheel. "You're right, Meems—

he doesn't . . . yet."

And then the spit comes back into my mouth

because even if Mr. Dell doesn't like us,

Papa said the words,

so they don't scare me as much.

Outside the car, light and dark and gray all stream by,

and I think, *Drip, drip, drip.*

Others

In Berkeley we lived in a two-bedroom house
next to my second cousins, Shelley and Sharon,
and Auntie Sachiko (who's really Mama's cousin)
and Uncle Kiyoshi.
There was no fence between our backyards,
so it was like we all lived in the same house.
Auntie let us live there
while Papa finished his schoolwork,
as long as
     he did repairs on their apartment building
     and Mama told people he was Italian.

Shelley and Sharon have Japanese middle names
like me: Akiko and Tomiko.
Sometimes they speak Japanese to Auntie and Uncle
and to each other,

and sometimes they combine English and Japanese.
My cousins taught me the Japanese words
that Mama would never say.
Sometimes we pretended we were Southern belles
who could speak Japanese—
"*Ohayō gozaimasu*, y'all."—
which made Mama and Auntie cry-laugh
out of breath.

Papa wants us to speak only English,
not because he doesn't like Japan
but because he says people get scared
when they hear a different language.

My cousins were my best friends.
We had other friends
whose parents or grandparents came from Japan
or China, Korea or India, Ghana or Germany or
Mexico.
We all understood our families' languages
and ate the foods of their countries.
It was like we were all in the *Other* check box,
having in common
speaking English,

being American,

and feeling that we didn't belong either in our
parents' worlds

or in this one.

But I am not Other;

I am

half my Japanese mother,

half my Black father,

and all me.

Winter

Quiet

sounds like winter in Vermont:

Snow taps the bare trees

Flames sing in the fireplace

Mama's slippers scuff the floors

The teakettle applauds to a boil

Hot water pours into a cup

A sip—

And Papa's "Quiet, please. I'm grading papers."

Karen and Kim

The two girls carry their trays to my table,
pocketbooks swinging from their elbows,
and sit on either side of me.
I didn't even need to invite them.

"We want to get to know you.
I'm Kim, I'm Karen," they say.
"You lived in California?" Karen asks.
I nod. "Uh-huh, in Berkeley."

"Did you go to wild parties there?"
   "Did you surf?"
            "How many movie stars did you
               meet?"
                     "Did you go to Disneyland
                        every weekend?"

I laugh and sip some milk.

"No. No. No. No," I say. "I didn't live in Hollywood.
I lived up north, near my mom's cousins."

"Can I touch your hair?" Kim asks.

It's a strange thing to ask, but I lean toward her.

She smooths the top of my head and runs her hand
down my braid.

Then Karen takes a turn, and says, "It's so curly."

Mama likes my hair pulled back tight and neat,
but a few curls always escape.

"I wish my hair was curly like yours," says Karen,
whose hair is straight and long and blond,
and I don't believe her.

"What nationality are you?"

I try not to sigh. "My dad is Black and my mom is
Japanese."

"*Japanese*-Japanese, or was she born here?"

"Japan. Hiroshima."

"Didn't we bomb Hiroshima?"

"Yes." *And the radiation is ticking in Mama's bones.*

"Do you know any Japanese words?" Kim asks.

"*Sukoshi dake*," I say,

and they look puzzled. "It means 'Just a little.'

My dad doesn't want us talking Japanese."

"What does he do to you if you talk
Japanese?"

"What? Nothing."

"I mean, I just thought . . ." Karen looks at
Kim.

My neck is prickling.

"Do you get a tan?"

I look at my arm. "Well, I get browner in the
summer."

"But not your palms, right? They still look
like ours."

Kim shows her hands to compare.

My lunch is done,

and so am I

with Karen and Kim.

Cooties

The first thing I notice about Stacey LaVoie
is her feet. We're standing in the corridor outside the
gym
and she's wearing red tights—and not the textured
kind.
Even I know that you stop wearing red tights after
fifth grade.
But I like that Stacey wears them anyway,
and that her big white toe sticks out of a hole
like a marshmallow.
She tries to cover the toe with her other foot,
but I've already seen it.
The next thing I notice is that black eyeliner
circles her whole eye
and ends with a little wing,
and she has pierced ears (Mama would never let me),
and earrings that dangle
just short of disobeying the dress code.

Miss Bonne, our gym teacher, is weighing us.
We are lined up in our stocking feet
outside the locker room.
Miss Bonne holds a clipboard in her hand
and a pencil in her mouth
while she slides the weights up and down the scale,
nudging them, zeroing in on the target.
"*Next!*" she calls.

"Watch out for the cootie hole," says the girl next to
Stacey
as we move up another person-space in line.
"The wha-at?" Stacey asks,
sounding like my cousins talking Southern,
only Stacey sounds real.
The girl points to a little hole in the wall
near Stacey's waist. "Don't touch it, or you'll get
cooties."
Stacey nods, making her dark hair bounce
like a girl in a Breck shampoo ad.
"I don't know what she's talking about," she whispers
to me. "Do you?"
"I think they're invisible bugs that you can catch."
The thought of cooties running all over me

makes me shiver, even if they're made up.

"Sounds kinda stupid," she says,

and I agree.

"Next!"

We move up, and now I'm next to the cootie hole.

Cooties are stupid, but I move away from the wall

anyway.

"I was new in September," Stacey says.

"We came from Georgia. My daddy teaches at the

college."

"Mine, too," I say, feeling happy

that we're both new

and both professors' daughters.

"It sure is different here, huh?" she says,

and shifts her weight to her other foot.

But she loses her balance

and falls onto me,

and I fall onto the next girl,

and on down the line.

"Stop pushing!" someone says,

shoving the girl who just knocked into her,

and the ripple swells up the line,

growing in strength and force

and intent.

When it comes back to me, I stop it

by falling into the wall,

against the cootie hole.

"Cooties!" the girl beside me says, and jumps away.

"I don't want to catch them!"

"Cooties!" say the girls. "Mimi's cooties."

All but Stacey, who yells, "It's my fault,"

over the chorus,

and touches my arm. "Now I've got them."

"Next!"

As stupid as cooties are,

I'm happy she took them from me.

But even though she made a big deal about rubbing

my arms

to catch the cooties, no one pays attention—

they just keep yelling

"Mimi's cooties, Mimi's cooties,"

as if they've been waiting to say that

ever since my first day at school,

and now they can.

Notes

Linda, the girl who sits next to me in history,
slips a note on my desk.
I tuck it into my notebook
and look at Stacey, who sits next to her.
She smiles, so I know her note says something good.
When Miss O'Connell turns to write on the board,
I unfold it quietly and read:

Want to do something after school?

She signed it *S*
with a long, loopy tail.

I could just nod at her,
but I've never passed notes before,

so I write back:

The drugstore!

I'll have to ask Papa
and figure out how to get home,
but I want to sit at the soda fountain with Stacey
and eat a sundae and look around the store.

The note is too small to explain all that,
so I just sign *M*
with no loops or flair,
then fold it up and slip it onto Linda's desk.
She covers it with her hand and passes it to Stacey,
who coughs and opens it.

"I'll take that, Miss LaVoie," Miss O'Connell says,
holding out her hand at the front of the room.
Stacey hands it to her,
then goes back to her desk without looking at me.

Miss O'Connell puts down her chalk and opens the
note.
"It's too bad," she says, "that instead

of sitting at the soda fountain this afternoon,
you'll be in my classroom."

I've never had detention before
and my neck prickles.
Now Stacey looks at me with a big-eye face
like she's pretending to be scared,
but I wonder if her heart is pounding
as hard as mine.

Detention

I had to tell Papa after school
about the notes and detention.
He blinked and said, "I'll be back in an hour."
The way he pressed his lips together
told me he was disappointed in me.
That stung more than getting caught passing a note.

Detention in Miss O'Connell's room
means sitting far away from Stacey,
and watching dust drift through the slanted sunlight,
and listening to kids' voices in the corridor
fade away,
and willing the red hand on the wall clock
to speed up
while Miss O'Connell helps a boy with homework.

When he leaves, Miss O'Connell says,

"An hour watching the clock is the longest hour you'll ever spend."

Stacey and I nod.

"But you can help yourselves. You can take five minutes off

for each history question you answer correctly."

I raise my hand. "Can we answer them together?"

Miss O'Connell sticks out her chin, and says,

"Okay."

Stacey and I smile at each other,

and I sit next to her.

Miss O'Connell takes out a stack of index cards,

shuffles them, and sits on her desk.

"First question—

What was the first battle of the American Revolution?"

I wink at Stacey, and say, "Lexington and Concord in April 1775."

"Yes," Miss O'Connell says. "You got five minutes off."

Thank you, Papa, I think.

She shuffles the cards again. "Hmm, let's see about
this one—

What does the first section of the Declaration of
Independence state?"

she asks,

and looks at Stacey.

"Do you know?" Stacey whispers to me,

and I answer, "All people are born with equal rights."

Miss O'Connell says, "That's another five minutes.

Now, let's see . . . ," she says, looking at the cards.
"Here's one—

How many times was Franklin Roosevelt elected
president?"

Stacey says, "I know that . . . four."

"Very good. I'm impressed," Miss O'Connell says.
"Last question—

I bet you girls can't get this one—

What was the name of the first

American-manned space mission?"

How easy can a question be? I think. "Freedom 7.

It was on May 5, 1961, and lasted fifteen minutes.

And Alan Shepard was the astronaut."

"Whoo-ee!" Stacey says.

"That's right, Mimi," Miss O'Connell says slowly.

"And for a bonus point—where was he born?"

She sits back on her desk and taps the cards in her palm,

waiting, I think, for me to get it wrong.

But I don't. "Derry, New Hampshire."

Miss O'Connell doesn't look impressed.

"These are not easy questions, Mimi.

Are you looking at the answers?"

She checks the backs of the cards,

but there's nothing there to see.

"I just like learning about the space missions."

"And her daddy teaches history," Stacey says.

"Well," Miss O'Connell says, sliding off her desk,

"you girls may go now. But no more notes."

We leave detention twenty-five minutes early.

"Do you want to meet my dad?" I ask Stacey

as we leave the building. "He'll be here soon."

"Can't now—my mother's here," she says,

and points to a yellow car at the curb. "Let's go to

the drugstore

over vacation," she calls over her shoulder,

then gets into the car.

I wave good-bye,

but I don't think she saw.

Science Project

It's my turn to talk to Mrs. Stanton
about my science project.
She shows me a book about lichen.

"But I don't want to do a report on lichen," I say
respectfully.
"That's fine, Miss Oliver. What do you want to do?"
I'm not afraid to tell her, but I am afraid she might
laugh,
like the homeroom kids on my first day.
"Something about the space program," I say.
She doesn't blink. "You mean Apollo?"
I nod and
hold my breath.

Mrs. Stanton takes the lichen book from me
and closes it. "That's a wonderful idea. What will
you focus on?"
  There are so many things to study about the moon—
    Training
    Building the rocket
    Living without gravity
    Navigating there—
  I know what I'll focus on: "The moon's topography
and its phases."

  Mrs. Stanton rests her chin in her hand for a
moment,
    then says, "All right."
  I smile, relieved.
  "Your report outline will be due next week," she says.
  "I'll help you with whatever you need, and
  I have a book on the subject at home."

  "Thank you," I say, and
  button my coat
  and pick up my books.
  But Mrs. Stanton doesn't say "You're welcome" or
even "'Bye,"

or shuffle the homework papers on her desk.
She keeps looking at me,
and I know we're not done.
"I hear you want to be an astronaut," she says.
"Yes." I put my books down
and wait for her to laugh
or tell me all girls want to be mothers
or teachers or secretaries or nurses.

Instead, she says, "I wanted to be a scientist.
I wanted to research viruses and find a cure for
diseases."
"But you didn't?"
She shakes her head. "My father said I'd be a
disgrace.
My mother wouldn't talk about it.
They said I'd never find a husband—
they didn't understand I could do both.
Then . . . my . . . I lost my husband. So I would have
had nothing."

"Don't you like being a teacher?" I ask.
She smiles. "I love teaching. If I can help my
students attain their dreams,

then I'm doing my job well. That makes me happy.
And when my husband died, I was happier than ever
to belong somewhere every day."
It's a big surprise to hear Mrs. Stanton talk about
dreams
and belonging,
but now I would do anything to make her happy,
because she wasn't able to attain her dreams,
and because . . .

"You didn't laugh at me," I say.
"Why would I laugh, Miss Oliver?
Our dreams are a serious matter.
When you take them seriously,
everyone else does too."
"You sound like my dad," I say.

Mrs. Stanton picks up her red pencil
and looks down at the papers on her desk.
"I will give you that book tomorrow."

Stars

On this clear and moonless night,
Mama and I wrap up in our winter clothes
and go outside to watch and listen.
The trees beyond our backyard form a torn-paper line
between the snow and this sky
filled with stars.

The snow glows lilac
as we step on its crust,
guided by faint starlight.
Mama and I don't need to talk.
We are in awe of the magnificence above—
impossible to understand, impossible to hold.
There were no skies like this in Berkeley,
where light from the cities chased the stars away.
Here I can't look long, deep, or wide enough

at the Vermont sky
on a new moon night.

I hold out my arms and twirl,
etching the sky above me in rings of starlight.
"Don't fall, Mimi-chan," Mama says, then
holds out her arms
and twirls.

February Vacation

"Pattress!" calls the boy next door,
breaking the winter quiet.
The brown dog leaps off the back steps
and disappears into the snow,
and the boy follows her out of the house.
Pattress appears
and disappears in the snow
again and again.
"Ruh! Ruh!" she calls, begging to play.

The boy packs a snowball and pitches it
way to the back of his yard.
Pattress chases it,
sniffs around where it should be,
then looks at the boy. She waits.
He throws another snowball

and another and another.
Her bark—insistent, joyful—
echoes off the surrounding woods.

She does her leap dance toward the long bump that
divides our yards.
When the snow melts, I'll find a fence under there.
The boy throws another snowball,
and—*whup!*—
it hits the empty turkey coop,
making it rattle.

He raises his arms,
either like "I'm sorry" or "Sock it to me."
I accept the challenge
and throw a handful of snow his way.
It doesn't even reach the fence,
and he bends over, laughing . . .
At me? This time,
I pack a snowball tight as ice,
wind up,
and pitch.
It explodes against a tree, spraying
the boy and his dog.

Soon we're having a snowball fight,
and we step closer and closer to the fence-bump
in the middle, laughing.
Pattress watches the snowballs sail past her,
biting and barking and leaping.

And just when I reach the fence,
ready to deliver the final blow,
Papa calls, "Mimi!"
his voice cutting through the laughter, slicing the
mood.

"'Bye," I say, and hold up my hand
empty of snowballs but coated in snow.
"'Bye," says the boy.

I go inside
and take off my boots
and shake the snow off my clothes.
When I look out the door,
Pattress and the boy are still standing by the bump.

The Soda Jerk

Stacey and I spin the stools at the soda fountain.

Then we sit on them and spin.

"You girls want something?" asks the man behind the

counter.

We stop spinning, and Stacey says, "Let me see,"

putting her finger on her chin as she studies the

menu.

He taps his fingers and looks at her while she

decides.

"What about your friend here?" he asks Stacey,

as if I'm not sitting right next to her.

I only have a dollar

and I also want to buy a headband.

"Can I have a hot-fudge sundae?" It's fifty cents.

"Oh, you speak English," he says. "I thought you was,

you know, a foreigner."

"I'm from California."

"Well you look kinda different."

I look big-eyed at Stacey in the mirror facing us.

She looks back at me the same way.

"You ready, miss?" he asks Stacey,

and she says, "One scoop of pistachio

and one scoop of chocolate."

He doesn't say anything about the way she talks.

After he goes away,

Stacey asks, "Do people always ask you stuff like
that?"

"You get used to it, kind of."

"I'd want to cuss them out. Don't you want to cuss
them out?"

"I just want them to stop."

"Well, I'd want to cuss," she says,

and then we both giggle.

I can tell Stacey anything

and she won't think I'm bad.

"You want to know what Mother calls him?" she asks,

her giggles like hiccups. "A . . . soda . . . jerk."

"Soda *jerk*?" I ask, my giggles choking me,

and she nods

hard, because she can't talk.

Then we spin some more,
but a lady in the cards section gives us a dirty look,
so we stop
and I make a pig face in the mirror.
Just like my cousins, Stacey makes one back.

Then the man brings our ice cream
but doesn't go away. I pick up my spoon
and he's still standing there.
"So, I have to know," he says,
"what are you?"
But just because he has to know
doesn't mean I have to tell him
anything.
I put my two quarters on the counter,
then slide off the stool.
"Wait for me," Stacey says,
and spoons a mound of pistachio in her mouth.

Outside, she says, "We know what *he* is—
a real soda jerk
minus the soda."

A Girl Who Twirls

Before today, I've only skated on an ice rink at a mall,
where you go round and round
in the same direction,
while organ music gives your glide its tempo.
There is always one girl
with a little skirt
who breaks away from the crowd and skates into the
center,
and twirls. She starts slow, throwing her arms out,
bent as if in worship to the ice and the force of
gravity,
and turns, her skirt flaring
and hands weaving invisible ribbons in the cold air.
Then, arms crossed over her chest, she spins
faster and faster into a blur,

drilling the ice
until she stops—
a flash of skates and spray.

I've always wanted to be that girl.

Skating Pond

The pond behind our yard has frozen
solid, and Papa said it's time to skate.
He brought Stacey and me home after school.
Mama gave us cookies and a thermos of cocoa
and told us to be very careful.
I know she wanted to come and watch
over us, but Papa said we'd never learn anything on
our own.
They can see us through the kitchen window
and the bare trees.

Stacey and I hang our skates over our shoulders.
They glint in the thin sunlight
as we walk the snowy path to the pond
that's ringed in dry timothy grass
and cattails poking out of the snow.
I brush off a stump

and we take turns lacing up our skates,
our bare fingers turning numb.

"Ready?" Stacey asks.
We tiptoe to the edge, where snow meets ice.
"Here goes," I say,
push off on one skate,
slide both together,
and push off on the other.
Stacey catches up, wobbly,
and we circle the pond slowly
side by side, our arms held out to steady ourselves
and each other.

After one time around, I know how this ice feels,
how frozen ripples change the sound,
and how to swerve around pebbles and twigs.
"Look—I can skate backward!" I call,
and show Stacey how I wiggle
into the center of the pond
like that girl at the mall rink.

"Twirl, Mimi!" Stacey says, clapping her mittens.
I laugh and hold out my arms.

"Watch me," I say,

and stop—

Because I'm not the girl with the cute skirt

and the ponytail that sticks out when she spins,

the perfect girl in the center

who everyone wants to be. I'll never be her—

No—

I'm the girl with cooties, the foolish girl

who wants to be an astronaut,

who eats by herself in the cafeteria.

I'm the girl all alone at the center

of attention,

not because of what I can do

but because of what I am.

Rendezvous

I wanted Stacey to stay longer,
but she has to be home for supper.
"You can take me back to school, Mr. Oliver," she
says in the car.
"It's no trouble to take you home," Papa says,
and asks for her address.
"It's hard to find . . . lots of twists and turns.
My mother is picking me up at school.
She'll be coming from the dentist's, anyway."
I don't know why Papa doesn't insist on taking her
home,
but he says no more.

When we get to school,
the sky and the snow are coral with dusk.
There are two cars in the parking lot,
but neither one belongs to Stacey's mother.

"Thank you very much," Stacey says, and opens her
door.

"We'll wait for your mom," Papa says.

Stacey steps out. "No, don't. She'll be here soon."

"But it's getting dark."

"I'm fine, Mr. Oliver," she says, her voice a note
higher,

her smile brittle.

Papa drums the steering wheel.

"I'll drive over there and wait until she comes.

Would that be all right?"

Stacey's face softens into a smile that looks like a cry.

"Yes. Thank you. I'm . . . sorr—"

Papa raises his hand, cutting her off. "It's okay.

You're welcome to visit us anytime, Stacey."

She shuts the door and waits at the top of the steps.

Papa parks near the track and turns off the lights
and engine,

and we wait. The sky grows fuchsia.

Stacey's mother comes soon, and Stacey gets in.

Her mother turns around to look at our car,

and they drive away,

two black silhouettes against the purple sunset.

Snowfall

Falling snow
is the sky
touching the ground.

Last night
the sky drifted
down—
flake
by flake
by flake,
so pretty and graceful
and quiet—
then it bent low,
poured out,
and lay down in itself.

Snow Day

This morning I wake up startled—late
for school!—and run down to the kitchen,
where Mama and Papa are eating together.
They only do that on Saturday.
"I'll be late!" I say, panicked that I'd broken
my perfect attendance.
"No school today," Mama says. "Look outside."
"Today's a snow day," Papa says.
We never had anything called a "snow day" in
California.
   Outside, the snow blankets our yard
in one even layer, all the way to the trees in the back.
Instead of falling quietly, now it races to the ground
hard and determined.
All the cars and tanks around Farmer Dell's house
are soft white hills.

Papa pushes back from the table.

"Get dressed, Meems. We have to shovel the
driveway."

"But it's still snowing," I say.

"Listen to Papa," Mama says,

setting a plate of scrambled eggs in front of me. "But
first, eat."

"Can we ask Mr. Dell for his snowblower?"

"I don't think so," Papa says.

Papa started shoveling at the house end of the
driveway

and moved toward the middle.

Mama and I started at the street end

and moved toward Papa.

Shoveling snow is like cutting up a cake—

you drop the shovel straight down to slice,

then push it flat underneath,

then lift and serve the snow to the side.

And repeat and repeat

unless the wind is blowing,

when all your hard work

ends up in your face.

I'm shivering in my sweat,

Mama is sniffling,

and Papa is puffing.

Down the road, I hear Farmer Dell's snowblower.

With it, we could clear our driveway in ten minutes.

Papa might not ask Mr. Dell,

but I will.

The Mouse Takes the Cheese

There are two hundred and sixteen steps
from our driveway to Farmer Dell's house.
I slip through the last forty-three
because he hasn't spread any sand or salt.
Maybe he doesn't want company.

I knock on the outside door,
and step back down to the walk
and wait. I hear heavy footsteps inside,
and the door opens
just wide enough for Mr. Dell's face to show.

"What do you want?" he asks.
"I'm Mimi Oliver."

I shift to my other foot. "We're neighbors."

"What do you want?"

"Well . . . we're shoveling, and there's a lot of snow,

and it's hard shoveling all that snow."

"Why'd ya come here, then?"

Farmer Dell has exactly the growl I imagined,

his nose hooks over his mouth,

and his eyebrows are thick and bushy,

like moths nesting on his forehead.

"I was wondering if . . ."

He stares. He's going to make me ask.

". . . we could borrow your snowblower."

"I don't give my things out to strangers. What do

you think I am—

a charity?"

"N-no."

"Is that all?" Farmer Dell asks, and starts to shut the

door.

"Wait," I say. "Is that boy here?"

"What boy?"

"The one who was playing with Pattress."

And just then, Pattress pushes the door open

all the way with her nose.

When she sees me, she wags her tail and barks
happily.

"Hi, Pattress! Do you want a snowball?" I ask.

Her ears stand up at *snowball*,

and she throws her head back, barking.

"So, is he home?" I ask.

"There's no boy here."

"Well, maybe when he comes home we can play with
Pattress."

Mr. Dell's eyes narrow.

"You go home now," he says, and shuts the door.

Pattress barks behind it

for her snowball.

I turn around and walk

two hundred and sixteen steps

back home. Mama and Papa

have finished the driveway,

so I shovel a path to the back door.

Consequences

Papa has never been so mad.
"I told you to leave him alone."
"Yes, Papa."
"I told you that some people don't want to be
friends."
"It's hard to shovel snow."
"There will be a lot harder things in life,
so shoveling a few inches of snow is good training."
"You mean a few feet."

"Mimi," he says, and takes my hands gently
to make me pay full attention.
"It is important that you understand.
We are new here. These people have lived in this town
many years. Their parents and grandparents
and great-great-grandparents were born here.

To them we are visitors—"

"You mean strangers?" I ask.

"To some people, we are. And you should know that
we might always be. But we still have to respect
them
and their ways."

"Then, let's go back to California," I say.

Papa drops my hands. "It's not that easy, Mimi-chan.

Besides, life wasn't perfect there, either."

"At least we didn't have to shovel snow."

Papa nods and chuckles

but gets serious again. "What should you have done
differently?"

When I was five or even ten

the answer would have been "Obey you and Mama."

But something's different now. That

is no longer the only solution.

Then Papa says, "If you can't tell me,

then go to your room and think about it."

But first, he hands me something from his briefcase.

"You want to take this with you?"

It's a *Life* magazine from January.

On the cover is that picture of Earth

taken from the moon.

I snatch the treasure and hug it tight. "Where did
you get this?"

"It comes to the department. Everyone else has read
it."

"You spoil her," Mama says. "How will she learn
consequences?"

Papa sighs and looks sheepishly at Mama. "Just this
once, Emi—

It might help her find the answer."

Tears on Glass

I try to blink away
Mr. Dell's scowling face
and his angry words
because I don't want to let him
make me cry.

Is it me that makes people here act so chilly?
Or is it my family?
We are American,
we speak English, we eat pizza
and pot roast,
and potatoes sometimes.

I feel like I have to be
twice as smart and funny at school,
and twice as nice and forgiving in my neighborhood

than everyone else
to be acceptable.
But everyone else can be
only half of that
to fit in.

Sad thoughts
just make you sadder if you let them.
I'm too sad now to stop them from taking me
with them.
I can't blink fast enough,
and when I press my face against the cold pane,
my tears turn to crystals.

Life in 1968

Last year, I knew about the Apollo program.
And I knew about Dr. King
and Bobby Kennedy—each time,
Auntie Sachi kept the TV on
to hear the news
and cried.
When we could watch *My Three Sons* again,
we knew life was back to normal.

But I didn't know about the two widows hugging
each other.
One is Mrs. Kennedy, and the other is Mrs. King.
They both lost their husbands.
They both must have cried through boxes of tissues,
knowing they'd never see them again.
So, did they both wonder,
when *Hogan's Heroes* came back on,
why their lives weren't back to normal?

A New Outlook

When this photo of Earth was taken from the moon,
I was in Berkeley
in California
in the United States
in North America
on Earth—
that same shimmering blue and white ball
twirling in blackness
and swirling with storms
that's in the picture.

But from space there are no borders
separating countries, states, people—only
land from water,
earth from sky,
dark from light.

Who I am and
who I become
depend on
what I look at,
what I listen to,
what I touch and smell and taste.

The Apollo 8 astronauts
watched Earth rise above the moon
and were changed.
Now I am seeing what they saw,
and it is changing me.

Spring
1969

Crocuses in the Snow

When Papa and I come home today,
Mama is standing by the side of the house,
hugging her coat around her and staring at the
ground.
"Look," she says, pointing at a purple flower
with petals cupped like hands piercing the snow.
"Is that a tulip?" I ask.
"It's a crocus," she says.
"Someone who used to live here planted a bulb.
And now the bulb is a flower."

Did the people who planted the bulb when the
ground was soft
hope to see the flower today?
Did they plant it before they knew they would leave
this house?

Or did they plant the bulb just for us,
like wrapping a present
and never seeing it opened?

When the ground is a blanket of snow
and ponds turn to ice
and everyone mummies up in scarves,
it feels like everything has stopped moving,
stopped breathing,
stopped living.
But secret things are still happening
in the deep below.
And when the time is right
they make their way to the surface
and explode in a surprise of purple.

Kimono

Mama uses her mother-of-pearl-handle scissors
to unwrap a package from Auntie Sachi.

"Look, Mimi-chan!" she says,
and slides her fingernails pink as blossoms
under the seam of the brown paper wrapping,
winds the twine around her fingers,
and ties a loose knot for safekeeping.
Then she carefully peels back the paper
covering a box.
"What's in it?" I ask impatiently.
"Wait," Mama says, and lifts the lid.
Inside is tissue paper.

"Auntie sent us tissue paper?" I ask.
"Let's see," Mama says, and opens the layers.

Underneath lies a length of silk
blue as a robin's egg
and a note.

> *Dear Emiko,*
> *You never treat yourself,*
> *so use this silk for a kimono*
> *for spring.*

"It's so pretty," I say, touching the fabric. "Isn't it?"
Mama just makes her Mifune face,
then gently folds up the silk
and puts it back in the box.

Relocation

In history, David Hurley says his uncle was killed
at Pearl Harbor, and it was a good thing
we bombed those Japs.
"We only did it to end the war," he says.
"We're the good guys."

"What do you say about that, people?" Miss
O'Connell asks.
I want to say what I heard from Auntie Sachi
about when she was a little girl and had to move to
Arizona.
I want to say maybe good guys
don't always do good things.
But I'm afraid to here in class.

"Mimi? Your family is Japanese," she says.

"Well . . ." I look around—

now I have to say something. "What about the relocation camps?"

"The what?" David asks.

"When Americans who were Japanese

had to leave their houses and live in camps in the desert

until the war was over."

"That never happened," David says, and

"I never heard of that," Linda says.

Auntie Sachi was there, so I say, "I'm sure it happened."

Miss O'Connell raises her hands for quiet.

"You have to understand

how the country felt at the time.

People were scared because

we were at war with Japan."

No one is saying "Yeah, that doesn't make any sense"

or "That sounds horrible" or

"How could they do that to people?" or even

"Is it true?"

They're just looking at me like I made it all up
and want to cause trouble. But Miss O'Connell says,
"You weren't alive at the time,
so you can't understand."

Now I wish I'd kept quiet,
the way Uncle Kiyoshi tells Auntie to be
whenever she brings up her life in Arizona.

Liars

Auntie Sachi wouldn't have given me the *Time*
magazine
    if Uncle Kiyoshi hadn't read it yet.
    She wouldn't have let us stay in their house
    if she wanted us to move out.
    She wouldn't say she loves both her daughters the
same
    and give one more rice.

    She is always truthful—
    so I know she didn't lie
    when she told me that during the war
    her family had to sell their house and grocery store
    and everything they owned in Sacramento
    and move to Arizona
    to live in a shack

in a camp
surrounded by barbed wire
with hundreds of other families
while her big brother fought in the army
for our country.

"You're a liar, Liar!"
              they're telling me in history.
"Show us where that's in our book,"
              they want to know.

It's not in our history book.
Maybe the people who wrote the book
forgot what happened to Auntie,
or decided to leave that part out
so no one would ever know what happened.
And after a while, everyone would forget
or call those who remembered
liars.

Moving Forward

Tonight I tell Mama and Papa
what happened in history.
"It's true, right?" I ask.
Mama picks up her plate and takes it to the sink.
"Mama, right?" I repeat, in case
she didn't hear me the first time.
"What is past is past," she says,
her back still to us. "We need to forget
and do our best now."
Papa has been watching her back
and now turns to me. "I agree with Mama
to a point. We can't dwell on what happened
but we need to remember
so we don't do it again.
It is our history,
but we don't want it be our future."

That is why I've decided
that even after I hand in my journal to Mr. Pease
in June, I'll keep writing in it.
I don't want to forget,
and I don't want someone else
to tell a different story about me.

Stacey's Birthday

At 3:36 this afternoon
Stacey will turn thirteen.
She wanted to come to the drugstore
and share a banana split to celebrate
the moment of her birth.

Today is also that soda jerk's day off,
so I feel okay being here.
But I wish I didn't have to think about
where not to go.

"What do you want for your birthday?" I ask.
I hope she says earrings, because
last week I'd bought her some, and
they're in my pocketbook.
She slices the banana with her spoon.

"I really want the Cream album
but Daddy says it's devil music, so I know I won't
get it."
"My dad has that one. It's cool."
"Then I'll have to listen to it at your house," she says,
tipping her spoon at me.
"Sure," I say, happy that she'll be over again.
We eat more ice cream
and I ask, "Are you going to have a party?"
It would be my first one here.
She pokes the banana with her spoon, then mumbles,
"I don't know . . . not today, anyway."

Then she turns bright red
and buries her face in her arm.
"I'm so sorry, Mimi," she sobs.
"Why—what happened?" I ask.
She lifts her head and wipes her nose with a napkin
and looks at me with red-rimmed eyes.
"I'm having a party Saturday,
but . . . didn't ask you."
"Oh," I say, guessing why.
"Mimi, you're my best friend,
but Mother—she's so old-fashioned.

I wanted you to be there so bad,
but I knew she'd say no."

This soda fountain hasn't been good to me.
And now I know
that Stacey wanted me to come here on her birthday
because I couldn't go to her house for her party.

The clock says 3:38. The moment has passed.
I put Stacey's present on the counter
and say, "Happy birthday."
But I don't say things like "I thought we were
friends" and
"I hope it rains at your party,"
because then I'd feel worse than I do now.
And because angry words are like minutes on the
clock—
once you use them, you can't get them back.

Light and Dark

My science project is finished,
a demonstration of the eight phases of the moon.
It is a Styrofoam ball
hanging from the lid of a shoebox.
I punched eight holes around the box,
one for each phase.
When I aim a flashlight at the ball,
it's like the sun shining on the moon.
You can look through the holes and see
the phases of light and dark:

New Moon
Waxing Crescent
First Quarter
Waxing Gibbous
Full Moon

Waning Gibbous
Last Quarter
Waning Crescent
and back to New

"This explains the phases very well," Papa says,
peering through a hole.
But Mama has noticed my waning crescent mood,
and asks, "What's wrong?"

"It's small and boring and flimsy.
I could have made this in fourth grade," I say,
and thump the Thom McAn shoebox
until the moon sways.
I will never win first prize with this moon box.

"What are you going to do about that?" Papa asks.
I snap off the flashlight, and the kitchen goes milky
dim
from the Full Sprouting Grass Moon outside.
I know what he wants from me,
and so do I:
"Make a better one," I say,
then sigh. "I just don't know how."

If I Had a Hammer

If I had a power drill
and a power saw
and a power screwdriver
and a vise for holding glued boards together while
they dry,
my moon project would be stellar.

But all we have are a rusty saw
and a screwdriver with a yellow handle
and a drill you crank by hand.

But every time I use those tools
to make a bigger, better, stronger moon box,
the wood splinters,
the corners bend,
my arms get tired from turning the crank,
and I think about switching my project
to lichens.

Poults

We have ten new babies—
ten turkey poults—
that Mama wants to raise
and "give away," as she says,
for Thanksgiving.
It's her way of saying
ten families will eat them for dinner.
But they are too cute to be eaten.

The poults will need to stay in the house,
where it's warm, until spring
because the coop out back
doesn't have the right heater.
So Mama set up the extra bedroom as an incubator
for the babies
and a cardboard gate to keep them in.

They clump at the gate

and peep whenever we talk or come down the hall

because I have spoiled them by sitting in the room

with them.

They climb all over me, looking for food and

cuddles.

"Don't name them," Mama says,

because then I won't let her give them away in the

fall.

But it's too late—

Rufus has short wings,

Bobo's claws are stubby,

and Shirley has a brown streak across her beak.

I wonder how I could bring them to my room

and let them sleep on my bed.

Math

Everyone in study hall is quiet, except for David Hurley,
who's telling Ann at the next table about his science
project,
    a water mill that has a motor.
    "I'm making it in wood shop. Mr. Sperangio lets me
    go in after school."

"Quiet, now," says Miss Borden, the librarian.
David and Ann glance at each other,
then back at their books.

I'm staring at my math book,
but trying to solve a different problem—
How to ask Mr. Sperangio in wood shop
about using the tools.

"That's not possible," he tells me
in his classroom after school.
"Shop is for boys."

"But I'm not talking about taking shop.
I just want to use the tools."

"These tools are dangerous."

"I'll be careful. I'm always careful."

"You haven't had any training."

"I can learn . . . really fast."

Mr. Sperangio lifts his hands,
and shakes them, like I'm a fly.
"Look, Miss Oliver, I'm sorry,
but girls can't come in here."

"So, the answer is no?"

"Yes,
the answer is no.

You'll have to find another way
to solve your problem."

Disappointment
ripples through me,
but I won't let it defeat me.
I'll find another way.

As I walk to the door,
David Hurley comes in
and slips on a pair of goggles.

Something Important

Mama has been invited to a tea
for the wives of professors at Hillsborough College.
When the invitation came in the mail last week,
she opened it and read it
like Mifune
and set it next to the napkin holder.

Today, Papa asks, "What are you going to tell them?"
"What is this tea all about?" she asks, looking at the
envelope
like it has poison ivy in it.
"Well, I've never been to one,
but I think you drink tea and talk with the other
wives."
"Oh. I don't need to do that, James."
"I think it would be good for you.

You would meet new people and
make some friends."
"I don't need friends—
I have you and Mimi
and the turkeys."
Papa says nothing. Mama says nothing
for a minute, and then,
Papa says, "If you knew
there would be someone at the tea you could talk to,
would you go?"
Mama sighs. "If it's that important to you, okay.
I will go to the tea."
Then Papa sits back in his chair and smiles.
"Thank you, Emi," he says.
It is that important to him.
And now I wonder who that someone will be.

April Vacation

Our yard is now a brown lake,
with patches of snow like stepping-stones.
The ground smells sour, like it threw back its covers
after napping for a hundred years.
Over there, in Mr. Dell's yard,
is that boy again,
the one I threw snowballs with over February
vacation,
the boy Mr. Dell told me didn't exist.

He tosses a Frisbee across the backyard,
and Pattress chases it, jumping and barking.
She catches it, runs in a wide circle,
drops it on the ground in front of the boy.
Then she backs off, barks again.
He tosses it,

then sees me standing here
by the turkey coop. I wait
for him to wave, speak, or walk away
like he did before.
I won't go first—
respecting his ways
and protecting my feelings.

I spread grain in the feeders.
I refill the waterers.
I check the inside temperature.
"Hi," I hear behind me,
and turn around.
He's standing
on his side of the fence.
Pattress is sitting, but
her tail sneaks a wag.

"Hello," I say, and wait.
"Are those chickens?" he asks.
"Turkeys."
"Oh." He stretches his neck for a better look.
"Wanna see them?" I ask.
The boy glances over his shoulder at Mr. Dell's
house,

then steps over the fence,

mud squishing around his boots.

Pattress jumps the fence and scampers ahead.

She nudges my hand with her nose

and I nuzzle it,

so cold and soft.

It's the first time I've touched her,

and she makes me want a dog of my own

just like her.

"How did she get her name?" I ask.

"Well, my uncle named her Patches,

but I pronounced it 'Pattress'

when I was little."

"I'm Mimi," I say to the boy.

"I know," he says. "I'm Timothy.

He's my uncle—my great-uncle,"

and I know *he* is Mr. Dell.

"I was about to clean the coop. Want to help?"

"Yeah," he says, and tells Pattress to stay.

Inside, the coop smells like hay and sawdust

and turkey poop.

The turkeys think we have more food

and mob us, gobbling.

We shuffle through them,
and they stream around us, gobbling.

I give Timothy a shovel. "I don't think your uncle
likes me."

Timothy scoops some spread and dumps it in the
bucket.

"I don't think he likes anybody
but Pattress."

We both shovel more, and I have more questions,
starting with "Why?"

Timothy shrugs. "He likes to be by himself."

"But you're here."

"My brother, Wesley, brings me here on school
vacations
to keep Uncle Raymond company.
My mom gets worried about him
all alone."

As we clean the coop,
I find out more about Timothy's uncle:
His wife died eight years ago,
he flew missions in World War II.
Now, when the weather is good, he goes flying

by himself. Or driving when it's bad.

And he has a telescope.

"It's huge," Timothy says. "You can see planets and stars."

When he says that, I drop my armful of hay.

"And the moon?"

Timothy nods.

"Can I see it?"

But now he shakes his head.

"Please?"

"He won't even let *me* touch it."

"I'll just look through it. Please-oh-please?"

Timothy shoves his hands in his pockets, then

says, "Maybe . . . when he goes out.

But no promises."

Just the thought is good enough

for now.

The back door of his uncle's house opens,

and Wesley sticks his head out and looks around.

Timothy doesn't call him. He just says, "I gotta go

now."

"You're not supposed to come here, right?"

He looks down and shakes his head no. "But I don't care."

After Timothy leaves, I realize he didn't ask me
all the usual questions.
Maybe he doesn't care about them.
And that makes me smile.

Inheritance

While Mama is at the wives' tea,

Papa and I are baking bread.

He uncovers the dough that's been rising in the
ceramic bowl

his dad—my grandpa—made long ago.

"And this bread is from your grandma's starter,"
Papa says.

It has lasted all these years,

longer than I am old.

"Tell me her stories," I say,

even though I've heard them all before.

As Papa spreads flour on the counter and kneads the
dough,

he tells me how she walked to the fields every
morning in summer

to work the crops,

and ate lunch from a tin pail,

and visited with neighbors on their front porches

when the day was done.

At school she shared a desk and a pencil

and wrote double between the lines to save paper.

He tells me how it feels to hold your breath

in an outhouse,

and I wonder if these are her stories

or his.

I hold my breath and pretend I'm there,

forgetting for a moment I'm in this warm kitchen

making bread with my dad.

Papa pinches off a handful of dough

and replaces it tightly in the jar.

This is our history, and I won't forget it.

Then he writes my name in the flour:

Mimi for the cicada's song;

Yoshiko for my *obāsan*;

Oliver for Papa.

"You have your mama's eyes," he says,

"and you have my stories."

April Moon

Timothy raps on the back door.
His cheeks are flushed in patches,
and his brown eyes sparkle.
"If you want to see the telescope,
you gotta come right now."

I pull him inside so he won't freeze
while I put on my shoes and jacket.
The kitchen smells like warm bread,
and he sniffs. "Mmm," he says,
and I tell him, "My dad's baking today."
"Your dad? That's cool.
All set?"

We run to Mr. Dell's garage, careful
not to slip in the muddy patches in our yards.
Timothy slides the heavy door shut behind us.

He leads me to the back of the garage,
past all Mr. Dell's machines,
where the windows are as tall as the ceiling
and curved at the top.
Planted near the windows is the telescope
pointed toward the sky,
like a kid gazing at the stars
in wonder.
Timothy bends over and looks in the eyepiece,
turns a knob, turns it some more,
then waves me to him.

"Can I?" I ask, the words shaking in my throat.
"You can look through it," he says,
"but *do not touch it*."
I clasp my hands behind me,
just to show him *I will not touch it*,
and bend over the eyepiece
and look

> at nothing
> but blue sky.

"Be patient," Timothy says.
So I look again and wait,

for something to come into view.

And it does—
at first I see an edge so bright I have to blink,
and curved like the peel of an onion—
the moon, so close.
It's peering back at me
as it slides across the circle of lens,
a waxing crescent

> dark,
>
> silent,
>
> enormous.

I see its pockmarks—
its craters and seas—
though it tries hard to hide them
in our shadow.

"I will touch you," I whisper,
but Timothy says, "I said no touching."
His words pull me back
to Earth.

Hope

All I saw when we came into this garage
was the telescope.
But now that the moon show is over,
I smell sawdust—
and turn around
to see a workbench
and power tools.
Could they be the other way to solve my problem?

"Does your uncle let you use those tools?" I ask
Timothy.
"Yeah, but mostly to fix things."
"Do you think I could I use them?" I ask,
and tell him about my science project.
He doesn't say

        girls aren't allowed,

        tools are dangerous,

you don't have any training,
it's impossible.

What he says is, "I'll show you how.
But only when he goes out."

There's a dark, enormous silence
between us. Finally I ask,
"Why doesn't your uncle like me? Why doesn't he
like my family? It's because
we're not like him, right?"
Then I wish I hadn't said that to Timothy,
my only friend besides Stacey,
in case he hadn't noticed we look different
and now he will see
and change his mind about me.
But I should have known better. I can trust Timothy,
because he shakes his head and says,
"He doesn't like anybody.
I don't know why, but
most of all, he doesn't like
himself."

Secrets

I don't want to keep secrets
from my parents, but since Mama hasn't asked
where I go with Timothy every morning
and why,
I'm not keeping a secret,
not really.

Every morning of vacation,
Timothy has knocked at the back door
after his uncle has left.
We go to the garage, and he shows me
how to use the tools for the next step
of my moon box.
Then I do each next step.
He's teaching me how to saw wood
and hammer and sand,

and reminds me, "Put on your goggles."
It's not cheating because I am doing all the work.

When we hear Mr. Dell's truck chugging up the
driveway,
    we hide my project
    behind a stack of tires in the garage,
    and I sneak out the back door.

Each day when I go home,
    Mama asks, "Did you have a nice time with
Timothy?"
    And I say yes, because it's the truth.
    But I still feel like I'm
    keeping secrets.

Weirdos

Today in the garage,
Timothy asks, "Remember when your father was
baking bread?"
I'm measuring a board and nod
instead of saying yes,
so I won't have to start over.
Then I mark the length with a pencil and ask, "Why?"
"Well . . . do you think he would teach me?"
"You want to make bread?"
Timothy looks down
and brushes the board. "I want to learn to cook.
Do you think that's . . . weird?"
"I like to hammer and saw. Do you think that's
weird?"
"No," he says, looking at me. "It's cool."
"Well, I think my dad would like to teach you. And

that would make us even."

"But I like showing you how to do this. I like
being around you. I mean,
I like you."

I'm glad the pencil rolls off the board just now,
so I have another reason to look down.

Sea of Tranquility

It's Thursday night, and Timothy and I
are more than halfway through April vacation
in different schools.
The moon box is almost done—
today we sanded it
then hid it, like always, behind the tires.
Tomorrow I'll bring it home and paint it black.

Tonight, Papa is showing Timothy
how to make a basic loaf of bread.
It's going to be round
because Papa says that's easiest,
and this is Timothy's first loaf.

While Timothy is learning how to bake,
I'm making a papier-mâché moon
by gluing newspaper strips to a ball

that Papa found in the cellar.
The hardest part will be shaping the craters and seas
so they're accurate.
But that part will also be the most fun
because I like their names,
which sound like poetry:

>   Sea of Tranquility
>   Kepler Crater
>   Sea of Vapors
>   Grimaldi Crater
>   Ocean of Storms, and
>   Lake of Dreams
are my favorites.

When the moon dries
I'll paint it white and different shades of gray
and hang it in the moon box.
My project will be like science meets art,
and it will win first prize.

Timothy slides the bread pan into the oven
and shuts the door.
His cheeks are flushed, like when he's cold or
embarrassed,
    but tonight I think it's how his happiness is showing.

"Thanks, Mr. Oliver," he tells Papa.

"Can we make something else . . .

tomorrow? I have to go back to New York on

Saturday."

Papa smiles. "I'll show you how to make an omelet.

It will come in handy when you go to college."

"Okay, but that's a long time away," Timothy says,

and Papa says, "Not really."

The bread will take an hour to bake. I hope

Timothy will want to stay until it's done,

instead of going out and coming back.

When he sits at the table and asks

how my moon is coming along,

I feel my cheeks flush.

Sign of Spring

I call it fireworks exploding yellow.

Papa calls it forsythia.

Mama just says *"Achoo!"*

Water and Dirt

Timothy and I are at the workbench
in Mr. Dell's garage.
A thread of spring weaves through the air.
Even though it's still April,
I get a whiff of May in Vermont—
light, sweet, and happy.

"Wesley's thinking of joining up,"
he says as we rub the moon box,
feeling for rough patches that need more sanding.
"He got a low draft number
and figures he's better off enlisting.
Then he'll be able to choose the branch."

I guess "Marines?" and he nods.
"My dad was a Marine.

He met my mom when he was stationed in Tokyo."
I can tell by the way Timothy concentrates on the box
that he doesn't want to hear how my parents met.
He says, "I don't want him to go to Vietnam."

I feel sandwiched by wars
and don't know what to say to Timothy, except,
"Are you coming back here this summer?"
"Probably. Hope so," he says.
I hope so, too,
and tell him that.

"This looks good," he says
about my moon box. "You did a good job."
"Can you help me carry it back?" I ask.
He opens the garage door—
and Mr. Dell walks in, blocking our way out.

"What you got there, Tim,
and who's that with you?" he asks.
I look at Timothy, who's flushed
now with embarrassment
or fear. He's not talking, so I answer.
"It's my science project,

and Timothy showed me how to put it together."
"He did,

did he?" Mr. Dell says.

"Yeah, Uncle Raymond."

"Well, now, you didn't happen to use my tools to put
it together,

did you? Because wouldn't that be cheating?"

"I don't think so," Timothy says.

"Oh, I think so. Especially when you're not supposed
to see this girl.

And now she's in my garage."

Mr. Dell looks at me with eyes colder than February.
I decide
I'm not as much afraid of him
as I don't like him.

"I'm sorry, Mr. Dell," I say,
so respectfully that Papa might be proud.
"I can carry it by myself, Timothy."
"I think you should," Mr. Dell says,
and steps away from the door.
I squeeze myself and the moon box through.

It's too bad we haven't painted it yet
because my tears are soaking into the lid

as I walk home through the mud.
I keep hearing Mr. Dell's words
and stop to catch my breath
when I realize
Timothy won't be coming over tonight
to make omelets.

One-Way

Why do all my friends here—
Stacey and Timothy—
come to my house
but never invite me to theirs?

Mama's Visitor

Mama met someone named Dr. Haseda
at the wives' tea.
(I wondered if she was the someone Papa talked
about.)
This afternoon Dr. Haseda came to our house
and brought lemon cookies as an *omiyage*.
Mama set them out in a pretty dish
and made a pot of tea.

Dr. Haseda was born in Los Angeles
and went to college in New York,
where she met her husband.
She teaches Japanese at the college.
Today she brought her daughter, Kate,
who is one year old.
At first, Mama called her Baby Cake

and soon we were all calling her that—
even Baby Cake, who can already say ten words.

Even though Mama said she only needs Papa and me
and the turkeys,
I'm glad she has a new friend,
because maybe then she will start to feel at home.

After we walked them to their car
and waited until they drove away, out of sight,
I said, "It was nice of her to visit you."
Mama smoothed her hair and said, "Papa asked her."
"Are you mad at him for that?" I asked, confused.
"No, Mimi-chan. That is love."

Spatial Reasoning

"This is a mistake,"
says Mrs. Golden, my guidance counselor.

She slides her glasses onto her nose
without taking her eyes from the test results in her
lap.

"This is your score on spatial reasoning."
Her fingernail points to
95 out of 100.

A mistake?

"Girls never score high on this test."
She takes off her glasses,
looks,

says nothing,

and waits for me to explain why

a girl

like me

would score as high as a boy

like, say, Andrew Dutton.

Does she think I cheated?

They showed you the pieces of something

taken apart

and you had to choose the way it would look

all put back together.

"I liked that test,

and it was easy."

"Something went wrong,

and you'll have to take it again."

Mrs. Golden shakes her head

and puts her glasses back on,

and I know the subject is closed.

Looking Forward

"While you're here," says Mrs. Golden,
"let's talk about your schedule for next year.
You'll be in eighth grade,
your last year before high school."

She pulls my schedule from the same manila folder
and puts it in my lap.
I skim the list while she reads:

English
Math *(Not algebra)*
US History—Civil War to Present
Art
Music
Physical Science—Intro
Home Economics
Gym
Clubs (optional)

"Do you have any questions?" she asks.

"Can I change my schedule?"

Her eyes narrow. "What do you want to change?"

"I want to swap home ec for shop."

Mrs. Golden sits back in her chair.

It squeaks.

She frowns.

"Why would you want to do that?"

"I want to learn how to make things in shop."

"But you learn how to make things in home ec."

"I already know how to cook and sew."

We look at each other. I breathe

and remember

drip, drip, drip,

respectfully. "So, may I?"

"I don't know

what you did in California

or what they taught you there

or what your family believes,

but that's impossible here, Mimi.

Girls don't take shop.
Really—do you see any boys
wanting to take home ec?"

I know this subject is also closed
for now.

Kind Of

The bell rings after English
and Stacey says, "Daddy finally let me get the Cream
album.
You want to come over today and listen?"
"I can't. Remember?"
"No, it's different. Mother did an about-face
about . . . all that. She asked me to invite you."
"What made it different?"
Stacey shrugs. "I think when she met your mother
at the wives' tea."

I don't know what Mama did or said
to change Stacey's mom's mind.
I want to say yes—but
I want to go
when I want to go,

not when Stacey's mom
says I can.

"Today's not a good day," I tell Stacey,
which is the truth.
"I have a lot of homework,"
which is kind of a lie.

"Sure?" she asks.
I nod. "Yeah."
I know she knows what I'm thinking
because she's my best friend
and can read my mind.
"Maybe tomorrow?" she asks.
"Maybe."
"Mimi, please don't be mad at me."
"I'm not."
Which is also kind of a lie.
"Okay, call me tonight," she says,
and looks kind of sad. I would be lying
if I said that didn't make me
kind of happy.

Moon Viewing

I'm trying hard not to believe
that kids in science class are ignoring me
while I present my project.

I try to ignore—

Ann Marie jiggling her foot
and picking at her cuticles

Bruce yawning
and stretching his mouth as wide as his arms

David getting out of his seat
and opening the window—

just when I ask
if anyone would like to look through the holes
and see the phases of the moon.

"Everyone, pay attention," Mrs. Stanton says,
then asks, "May I look?"

I'm trying hard to smile
in front of the class
without breaking apart,
and pretend I don't see—

    while Mrs. Stanton gazes at the moon,
    unaware—

that kids are making squint-eyes at me.

The A Group

Only ten science projects can go
into the A group.
They will be judged for first, second, and third prizes
in the Science Groove
by college students who are studying the same topics,
and by Mr. Donovan, the school superintendent,
who invented a spray that makes your hair smell clean.

And guess which project
made it into the A group?
Guess!

Someone wasn't ignoring me on Tuesday
when I presented my project.
Thank you, Mrs. Stanton,
for the A group
and the A plus!

Best Friends Always

I'm not mad at Stacey anymore,
and I hope she isn't mad at me
as I dial her number tonight.

"I'm sorry," I say, and
right away she says, "I'm sorry, too.
Best friends?"
"Always," I say, feeling lighter
now that my anger has disappeared.

"Do you want to come over on Saturday
and get ready for the dance together?" she asks.

My heart still has a little bruise
where her mom didn't want me at her house,
so I ask, "Can you come here instead?"
"It's really okay, Mimi," she says.

"Please?" I ask.
And when she comes back to the phone
and asks, "What time?"
that bruise heals
a little more.

Dress, Hair, and Makeup

Auntie and I used to watch
Shindig! and *Hullabaloo*
and sometimes Dick Clark
and dance.
She let me wear her white lipstick
and her go-go boots
as we did the Pony.

Tonight is my first real dance.
School calls it Spring Fling,
but everyone else calls it Spring *Thing.*
Stacey came home with me after school.

Mama made tempura—because she knows people
like tempura—

and meat loaf, in case Stacey didn't like tempura.

We had rice, and Mama asked if she wanted

potatoes.

Stacey smiled and said, "We ate rice in Georgia, too."

Now we go up to my room. I open the windows

because the warm May air puts me in the mood

for getting ready for my first dance.

Stacey's dress is made of dotted swiss.

It has a white bodice and a violet skirt,

with a thin, white ribbon and a tiny flower at the

waist.

She got it at a store called Bonwit Teller in Boston.

Her hair is in big curlers all around her head,

and when she puts mascara on her eyelashes,

her mouth opens, the way mine does when I look at

the moon and stars.

Mama made my dress

from the robin's-egg blue silk

that Auntie Sachi sent her for a kimono.

But Mama said she'd rather make a dress

she can see on me

than a kimono

she can see on herself

only in a mirror.

She said, "Besides, finding a *gofukuya* here to make a kimono

is like finding snow in Honolulu."

"Your mother is so talented," Stacey says,

running her fingers through a pleat in my dress.

"Does she make all your clothes?"

"Most of them," I say, feeling guilty

that I wish my dress

had come from Bonwit Teller.

Now Stacey's doing my makeup.

"Not too much," Mama had told me yesterday.

"You're beautiful enough already."

My skin is too dark to wear Stacey's liquid foundation,

but she pats blusher on my cheeks,

and smooths Vaseline on my lower lip with her pinkie.

"Go like this," she says, pressing her lips together.

And when she stands close to me to draw on my eyelids,

her breath smells like toothpaste and tempura shrimp.

"Now your hair. Let's make it loose."

"No—Mama likes it pulled back tight."

"She won't mind just for tonight," Stacey says,

then undoes my braid and combs my hair with her
fingers.

She rubs a dab of goop in her hands

and runs them through my hair again, and says,

"Now your curls are making themselves known."

She clips the sides together at the back of my head.

"What do you think?" she asks

as we stand side by side in the mirror.

I'm afraid to love what I see—

afraid it would be too vain

to think the girl with the blue dress and shiny lips

and hair curling around her shoulders

is pretty, so I say,

"You are so talented."

We go downstairs

and Papa takes pictures of us,

together and separately.

Mama holds out her wedding pearls

and tells me to turn around.

They are cold on my neck, and I

feel like I've just grown up five years.

"The boys won't have a chance around you girls,"

Papa says,

and Stacey and I look at each other and say, "Eww."

But I know what the boys think of Stacey

and how they're afraid to talk to her

because she's so pretty and has that accent

as fragrant as lilacs.

We put on our shoes at the door,

and Papa presses a dime into my palm.

"Just in case you need to call," he says.

I don't understand

because he's picking me up after the dance.

When we drive past Mr. Dell's house,

I wish Timothy were here

to see me all dressed up for my first dance.

Spring Thing

When we go into the gym,
the band is playing "The Mighty Quinn"
so loud
that we have to shout in each other's ears.
The drums beat from my soles to my chest,
and I'm so excited
or nervous
that giggles go down my throat,
and I feel that something brand new
is going to happen tonight.

There are streamers along the walls, and the lights
are dim,
but everything—
earrings, barrettes, and even buttons
on the boys' shirts—glitters.
The air smells like roses and Tabu and Canoe
and Right Guard spray.

Girls with ribbons in their hair
are talking to girls with flower earrings
and boys who scratch their necks.
Somewhere beyond that wall of kids,
people must be dancing.

Stacey starts to move her arms and legs,
and I dance with her.
"Hey, you're good!" she shouts in my ear,
and I smile. It's because of Auntie Sachi
and Dick Clark.

A few seconds later, a tall boy in eighth grade
taps her on the shoulder.
She twists around and he says something in her ear.
She nods. "Be right back," she says to me,
and they go through the wall of kids.
The band switches to "Love Is All Around,"
so they must be slow dancing.

I turn around, looking at the girls and boys
talking, hoping someone will see me and smile
and wave me in to their group.
But no one does.

At the refreshment table I get a Tab
and back up to the wall near the girls' room,
and smile at people. Some smile back,
but they all have something important to do.

I finish my Tab and turn to put the can in the trash,
when someone bumps me,
knocking me against the table,
and moves on.

The kids behind the refreshment table don't seem to
notice
what happened to me,
but they see the tipped-over cans and bottles
and quickly line them up again.
The band is playing "Girl Watcher." I am not that girl.
I'm like that part of the moon that the crescent curls
around—
in shadow,
invisible.

Deep in my pocketbook
I find the dime Papa gave me.

Science Groove

School will be over in two weeks,
but we still have lots to do before then.

Today
we brought our science projects to school
for the Science Groove.
Papa carried my moon box,
and I carried my poster and report
and the flashlight and extra batteries
to the gym,
where many long tables were set up
to hold the displays.

Tonight
the teachers and parents and families
and anyone else
will come to the gym,

look at the projects, and ask questions.
Mrs. Stanton said there isn't much to do in
Hillsborough,
so everyone in town comes to the Science Groove.

Tomorrow
the judges will look at the Group A and B projects
and read our reports
and ask us questions.

Papa said my project is in a good spot,
at the end of the table,
where you can see it from the entrance to the gym.
People are coming by
and looking through the holes at the moon
and asking questions, like
    "Why did you do this project?" and
    "Do you like the moon?" and
    "What nationality are you?"
(But mostly they ask about my project.)

The big difference between Group A and Group B
is that Group A wins the awards.
David, who made the water mill in wood shop,
is next to me. He's in Group B

but thinks he should be in A,
and has told me many times tonight
in many different ways—like

    "How is a box with holes better than a water mill?"
    "Your father made that, right?"
    "I'd be in Group A if you didn't move here," and
    "People should stay with their own kind."

It's funny
how other people get to decide when I'm invisible
but I can't make them disappear.
So I turn around and pretend to straighten my
poster,
    when someone behind me says,
    "Well, well. That's a good-looking box.
    Did you make that all by yourself?"
I nod, and turn around
to see Mr. Dell.
My heart thumps at the surprise
of seeing him at school,
until I remember the Science Groove is public.

"Hello," I say carefully.
"Mm-hmm," he says with a little nod,
and walks on down the aisle.

No Words

WHO
took the moon out of my moon box?

And

WHY
would anyone do that?

I have no words left.
They've drifted away
into the vast, expanding
loneliness
of space.

But I still have lots of tears.

Full Missing Moon

Mr. Donovan and Mrs. Stanton let me stay in the
Groove
   even though my moon is gone
   and I couldn't show the judge
   the best part of my project—the moon and its
phases.
   He could only look through the holes of the moon
box
   and imagine how my moon would look
   with the flashlight shining on it from different angles.
   He could not know how beautiful my moon was
   and how hard I worked on it.

   The worst part about all this—
   worse than having my moon stolen—
   is that I'm now in Group B,

and I won't win first prize.
And David's water mill
moved into my spot in Group A.

David won't look at me
as we stand beside our projects,
waiting for the results.

Bad Dreams

You know
those bad dreams
that make you glad
they were only dreams?

I wish
I could wake up
from bad days.

Learning Japanese

Tuesday after the Science Groove,
Karen and Kim sit at a table in the cafeteria
and hang their pocketbooks on the chairs.
I take my tray over to them, and ask,
"Do you still want to learn Japanese?"
"Yes," they say, nodding so hard the table teeters.
"Teach us some words."

"Okay, here's one—*baka*."
"*Baka*," they repeat. "What's that mean?"
"Well, it's hard to translate . . . but it's a sign
of respect," I say,
and hold my hand over my mouth like Mama.
This is fun.
"Like, you say it to teachers?"
"That's right. And your parents."

"Is that what your mom says to your dad?"
"All the time," I say,
and pick up my tray to go.
"Sit with us," they say,
and smile.

That's when I stop laughing
and almost tell them the truth.
That's when I wish I could tell them
how much it hurts and how lonely I feel—
which is why I just taught them a word
my mom would be ashamed to know
that I know.

Party Snacks

Next Friday is the last day of school, so
Mr. Pease is holding up a sheet of paper
in homeroom. "Quiet down, students.
Please sign-up for our end-of-the year party.
You can bring any kind of snack,
like brownies or potato chips."

He gives the paper to Robert
in the first seat in the first row.
When it comes around to me,
I write *Sushi*, even though I haven't asked Mama
if she'll make it.
Then I look at what I've written
and think of the faces
the kids will make when they see the sushi
and the tone of their voices

when they ask, "You eat raw fish?"
even though that sushi would have cooked shrimp
and eggs
and vegetables,
or maybe hot dogs.
So I cross out *Sushi*
and write *Chocolate chip cookies.*

The End of the Beginning

It's the last day of school.
The last day of my seventh grade.
And the last class of my last day
of seventh grade
is English.
Mr. Pease is handing back our journals.
When he gives me mine,
he holds it a second longer,
and says, "Very good, Miss Oliver."

I open it
and flip through the pages.
Mr. Pease wrote things like *Very good*
and *Very observant*
and *Really?*
And he marked spelling mistakes.

I skip past the pages
where I know I've said things
that weren't kind or respectful
about other people.

But when I get to the last page,
I see a big, red A+
and next to that:

> *I enjoyed reading this very much*
> *and I do know you better.*
> *Please keep writing poetry—*
> *you have a gift.*

I'm glad it has helped Mr. Pease know me.
But even better,
it has helped me know myself.

Summer
1969

The Question

Papa's last class ended today,
and college is over for the year, too.

We're eating supper on the picnic table in the
backyard
because the air is warm and soft
as the sky turns colors.
The quarter moon is a shell on the sunset's shore.

Papa puts down his fork
and leans his elbows on the table.
I slap a mosquito on my arm
and wait for him to talk.

"We have a decision to make," he says.
"I've been here for two semesters,

and you and Mama have been here almost six
months.

If it's not working out for you, we can leave.

Someone offered me another teaching position
today, in Texas."

"Does that mean we'll have to move again?" I ask.

"Yes," Papa says.

Mama stays quiet.

"Do we have to make up our minds now?"

"I'll need to know by the end of July

at the latest," Papa says. "And the question is:

Do we stay or do we go?"

Pie, the Moon, and Stacey

Today is Flag Day,
and Mama hung a flag on the front porch.
It curled in the breeze like a cat's tail.

Today is also my birthday.
We had lemon meringue pie
instead of cake because that's my favorite,
and Neapolitan ice cream,
because I can never decide which flavor I like best.
Papa turned on the sprinkler,
and Stacey and I did ballet leaps and bunny hops
through the spray.

Then Mama and Papa gave me a hi-fi record player,
and Stacey gave me the new Temptations album.

I asked them if they had planned it that way,
and everyone laughed and looked away
so I knew the answer was yes. It made me happy
that they had talked behind my back
in a nice way.

Then Timothy came over with a present.
He glanced at Papa and handed me a little box
with COTTLE's written on the lid.
Inside was a happy silver moon on a chain.

Stacey is staying over tonight.
It's my first sleepover
since Shelley and Sharon and I slept on their living
room floor
and watched *The Flying Nun* and *Bewitched*
the night before Mama and I left Berkeley.
Stacey and I are sitting at the two window seats
and talking through the screens. We can hear each
other
inside and out.
"Just think," she says,
"you've been on this earth thirteen years."

I look up at the sky and wish
new moons had names, like full moons do.
I will call tonight's moon New Birthday Moon.

When I opened the box from Timothy today,
he said, "Look—I found your moon."
I am thirteen today,
and the moon that disappeared
from my science project
and from tonight's sky
is here, dangling at my throat.

Magicicadas

Because of the New Birthday Moon tonight,
the stars are full twinkling brilliance.
Later, after the mosquitoes have disappeared,
Stacey and I will go outside and twirl.

"Why did they name you Stacey?" I ask through the
screen.
"Mother said a nurse named Stacey helped her
after I was born," she says. "I was a preemie,
and Mother and Daddy thought I was going to die."
"But you didn't, thank goodness," I say.
"I'm too tough. When I get old,
and am about to go, I'll kick death so hard
that it will go away."
That's another reason I like Stacey.

"How did you get your name?" she asks.
"My dad said that when I was born,
Mama thought I cried like the cicadas' song—
mee-mee—
and made her think of home. Japan."

"We have cicadas in Georgia.
I love the sound. It's a summer sound,"
she says softly, like she misses them, too.

Then I say, "I read there are cicadas
that live in the ground for years.
They're called *magicicadas*,
and when they're ready, they all burst out at once
and fly, blocking out the moon."
"Mother saw that once," she says. "I wish we could
see them here."

I look into the part of the sky
where the New Birthday Moon should be,
and say, "They wait until just the right time."

Apollo 11

Timothy comes to our house at nine o'clock this
morning
    to watch the launch of Apollo 11,
    which will carry three men to the moon.
    Papa says if we don't see this historic event,
    we will regret it the rest of our lives
    because he'll never speak to us again.
    But he doesn't have to tell me that,
    even if it is a joke.

    Mama brings me a tube of butcher paper,
    which I unroll on the living room floor
    to make a map of this historic event.

    I draw Earth
    and the Saturn V rocket steaming on the launchpad.
    I draw a window near the top,

and Neil Armstrong, Buzz Aldrin, and Mike Collins
waving.
"One day that will be me," I say,
and Timothy and Papa say, "May-*be*."
Mama says, "Just be careful."
Then I draw the moon
two hundred thousand miles away from Earth.

"Good luck and Godspeed," says the control tower
to the astronauts,
and Neil Armstrong answers, *"We know it will be a
good flight."*

The countdown begins,
and the numbers on the TV change every second—
as my heart pounds for the astronauts—
*". . . five . . . four . . . ignition sequencing starts . . .
two . . . one . . .
zero."*
Fire and smoke billow from the launchpad
and Saturn V leaves the ground.
"Liftoff. We have a liftoff."

The flaming fuel putters, pushing Saturn V higher
and higher in the sky, through the clouds.

I feel power, speed, and the drag of gravity.

The rocket looks like it's traveling sideways.

The boosters break away,

and now the ship becomes a bird with fanlike wings,

now a faint dot.

"You're looking good," says Houston.

Timothy and I pick up each end of the butcher paper

and carry it up to my room.

We tape it on the long wall.

I draw a dotted line for the flight path,

from Earth to the moon

and back—

for the eight days the astronauts will be in space.

And I draw a solid line for their trip so far.

I will draw them

all the way home.

Room of Kings

In Papa's study
a picture of Jesus hangs on the wall,
so when the sun rises in the morning
his blue eyes sparkle.

Across the room is a picture of President Kennedy.
He looks straight into the camera
with one stern eye
and the other eye trying not to smile.

Next to him is a new frame,
with five black-and-white pictures, each in its own
pane:
> The Reflecting Pool's walkways teeming with
> people
> Signs for *We Demand Equal Rights Now!*

Papa with two friends, looking young and
   dorky
Dr. King raising his arm above the crowd

"Did you go to the march?" I ask, peering at Dr. King,
who might have been saying "Let freedom ring!" at
that moment.
   "It was incredible, and it was a safer thing to do."
His heart was in Birmingham and Selma, he adds,
but he had a wife and a little girl,
and was studying for his PhD.
   "Safe is a cop-out, but I had to think of you and
Mama
   and my own dreams."

So he and his friends drove from Berkeley to
Washington
   without stopping.
They ate food that Mama had packed,
and switched drivers every six hours.
"This is big, big country, Mimi," he says,
like he forgot how Mama and I came to Vermont.

Then he tells me the air on that August day
   felt thick with heat and determination

smelled like baby powder, Old Spice, and grit,
sounded like clapping and harmony, a
    million footsteps on the same path
tasted like hot dogs and hope.

Papa opens his desk drawer and takes out a
button—
March for Freedom and Jobs—
and tapes it onto the new frame. He says,
"Even now, that day reminds me
that raindrops are stronger than hammers."

Remember This Night

The Sea of Tranquility slides under the window of
Eagle, the lunar module.
The moon's surface gets closer, bigger,
and Eagle lands.
We wait
to see a man walk on the moon
for the very first time,
ever.

Mama serves us potato salad and rolled-up ham slices
on TV trays
while we watch the fuzzy black-and-white pictures
from so far away.

She brings me a Coke with ice
so I can stay awake

to see the first man walk on the moon.
But I don't need caffeine to stay awake tonight.

Papa says, "Remember this night."
Mama says, "To tell your children,
my grandchildren."

It's almost eleven o'clock
and Eagle's hatch is open.
I stare at the TV
as Mama passes the bowl of popcorn.
Neil Armstrong stands on the ladder,
which he says is sunk one to two inches into the
moon's surface.
Then he steps into the dust
and touches a brand-   new   world.
He says,
"One small step   for man
    One   giant leap   for mankind."

Papa says, "Those words just traveled around the
world."

Soon, Buzz Aldrin squeezes out of the lunar module

like a person being born all over again,
and the two astronauts hop around
like moon kangaroos.

"It has a stark beauty all its own," Neil Armstrong says,
"like the high desert of the United States."
The lunar surface does look beautiful, but
I wonder if he has ever seen
winter in Vermont.

The Real Thing

The astronauts have returned to the lunar module
and are sealed inside.
Watching them on TV was one thing,
but not the real thing,
so I go to the backyard
to look at the moon in the sky,
which tonight is waxing crescent, almost
first quarter,
showing the shore of the tranquil sea,
where the astronauts are resting in Eagle.

In the silence of this magical night,
low voices drift from Mr. Dell's yard
and dark figures move in the pale light.

When my eyes adjust,
Mr. Dell and Timothy are huddled over the telescope.

My heart thuds—

they're watching the moon through the telescope.

Can they see

the lunar module gleaming in the sea,

the flag planted in the dust,

Columbia orbiting the moon, waiting to rendezvous?

Timothy moves away from the telescope.

I flap my arms to catch his eye,

and he waves behind his uncle's back,

then points to the moon.

I wave back and point and smile.

Pattress sees me and runs to the fence

and barks hello.

Mr. Dell steps back from the telescope,

straightens up and sees me.

"Get back!" he barks

at Pattress,

at me.

My heart hurts

over Pattress,

Timothy,
the telescope.

Papa said to remember this night.
But he doesn't have to worry, because
I will never forget it.

The Answer

It's time to decide
whether we will stay in Vermont
or move to Texas.

Papa has called Mama and me to the picnic table
to take a vote. The air smells like ozone from the rain,
and the Full Buck Moon glows through a veil
of clouds.

"What do you say, Emiko?" Papa asks.
"Up to you," Mama says.
"Not this time," Papa says. "It's up to all of us."
Then he touches my arm.

I knew this moment was coming.
I don't want to go to Texas.
I don't want to stay here either.
I want to go back to Berkeley

and be with my cousins. But I have a feeling
my cousins wouldn't be the same,
and everything would be different,
because I'm different now. I have changed in
Vermont.

Papa's waiting for my answer.
Didn't he say to remember the past
but keep looking forward?
If we leave Vermont now, I'd never know
what it held for me.
I want to find out, so I vote
"Stay."

"Now, Emi," he says to Mama.
She looks at me and then at Papa
and says, "Stay, too."

Papa rubs his hands together,
almost clapping. "It's unanimous," he says.
"Good things are in store for us here—
I feel it."

Good News and Sadness

Timothy and Pattress cross the fence
while I'm feeding the turkeys.
"I have some news," he says,
taking the bucket of grain from me.
He pours it into the feeder.

"Is it good news?" I ask.
"I think so."
"I have news, too."

"You first," Timothy says.
I tell him, "We're staying in Hillsborough."

"Cool," he says. "Because my news is
I'm staying here till next June."
"That's great news," I say, and smile.
But Timothy's eyes look sad.

"Right?"

"Sure," he says, and shrugs,

and keeps looking at me like he needs more

than a smile.

We give the turkeys fresh water,

and Timothy helps me lock the pen.

Pattress has been sitting outside all this time

and wags her tail when we come out.

Finally I ask, "Why are you staying here?

Doesn't your mother want you home,

now that Wesley's in Vietnam?"

Then he tells me a little

about his life in New York

and why he's staying with his grumpy uncle.

"My dad and mom are divorced.

He left us when I was three."

"Do you remember your dad?"

"Not really. My mom and Wesley

have told me stories,

but now I don't know if I remember him or the

stories.

Mom thinks I need to be around someone

who can be like a father.
She doesn't like that I like to cook."
"My dad likes to cook."
"I would tell her that
if I didn't have to keep it a secret
that I come over here."

"You have to keep lots of secrets. Isn't it hard
to keep them all straight?"
"I like coming over," he says.
"It's one of the only reasons
I even want to stay with my uncle."

Then I say what Papa says all the time:
"You are welcome to visit us anytime."
Timothy smiles finally.
"I wish I lived here. I wish
I had your family."
"I don't think you'd want to be in my family.
It's not always easy."
"My family isn't easy, either."

Now I know
that what Timothy needed more than a smile
was for me to hear his story.

I give him a hug
for the first time,
and he hugs me back
as if he has wanted to forever.
It feels good. And now I'm glad
my family voted to stay.

Language

Dr. Haseda has come to visit us again
with Baby Cake, who
has grown up so much since April.
Now she walks without lurching
and has lots more teeth.
I take her outside and blow bubbles
so Mama and her friend can visit alone.
Kate chases the bubbles and pops them
with her fingers and her face,
and laughs and screams
and falls down.

Timothy crosses the fence
and gives Kate pony rides on his back.
She grabs the neck of his T-shirt
and his ears
as he neighs and whinnies through the grass.

She wants to ride on Pattress, too,
who would let her,
but we say no,
and blow more bubbles.

Then Timothy has to leave,
and Kate and I go inside, where our mothers
are drinking tea with lemon and eating ginger cookies
that Dr. Haseda brought.
She gives one to her daughter.
And when she sets Kate on her lap,
Mama presses her hand over her heart
and looks at me.

"I am thinking of offering a class in the tea
ceremony," Dr. Haseda says to Mama
    in Japanese.
    Mama sets her teacup in the saucer. "Did you know
    I am certified to teach *osadō*?"
    "My, my," Dr. Haseda says. "I don't suppose you'd be
interested in teaching my class."
    Mama looks at her teacup to hide her smile. "I might
be.
    I'll need to talk to my husband first."

This is Mama's way of hiding her glee.
"Of course," says Dr. Haseda,
who puts her teacup down and gathers her daughter.
She knows Mama's answer will be yes.

I would not be able to explain to Timothy or Stacey
or anyone else in Hillsborough how
I understand the language
behind their words.

Tilling

Papa nudges his dinner plate,
but Mama doesn't take it to the sink right away.
When I get up to leave,
she says, "Stay, Mimi-chan,"
and starts telling Papa about Dr. Haseda's visit,
what a nice person she is,
and how big Baby Cake has grown.

Papa nods patiently.
I'm holding my breath for the punch line,
because Mama's way is to feel out the mood,
till the soil before planting the seeds.

Finally Papa asks, "What else?"
kindly.
"She wants to introduce students to tea ceremony
this fall."

"And she asked you to teach," Papa says.

"That's right."

"Can you handle it?" Papa asks. "There are turkeys
and the house and the family."

"Up to you," Mama says.

"Do you want to teach?" Papa asks.

"What do you think?" she asks.

Mama's face has no expression—

not joy or sadness or anticipation.

She stares at Papa, waiting.

"It's fine with me," he says,

and smiles, as if making a decision like that is a
burden

he carries with reverence.

Mama's mouth twitches into a smile

she can't stop,

so she takes Papa's plate to the sink.

"Oh," she says, turning around,

"something else. . . . She asked if Mimi can babysit
for Kate

on Saturday night."

"Me, babysit?" I ask.

I can't keep my smile from taking over my face

or my squeals from bouncing off the walls.

"You're certainly not your mother," Papa says,

laughing.

I look from him to Mama. "Can I?

I want to do it.

And I can handle it."

"I'll ask her for the details," Papa says,

"and tell her yes."

And that's how Mama and I get our first jobs

in Hillsborough on the same day.

Babysitting Baby Cake

Dr. Haseda opens the fridge. "Here
are her bottles." They're all lined up on the middle
shelf.
"Always heat them in warm water," she says
just like a teacher.
"But she just ate
and shouldn't be hungry. In fact,
she'll probably sleep straight through for you."
"So I won't get to play with her?" I ask.
"Not tonight, but maybe next time,
if you want to come back."

Her husband, Rick, is a sculptor,
who works in their garage.
He has long hair and a bushy beard.
At first, he and Dr. Haseda didn't seem to fit.
But after five minutes I knew they were perfect for
each other.

They're going to a movie at the college.
"We won't be late," Dr. Haseda says,
and shows me a number next to the phone.
But I say, "I'll be fine . . . we'll be fine.
Kate and I are best friends. Don't worry. Have fun."

After they leave, I go to Kate's room
to check on her. She's lying on her side
and her mouth is open just a little.
She smells like milk and baby shampoo,
and her lips are moving like she's chewing.
She has kicked off her blanket, so I pull it back over
her,
and I go back to the living room and look at the
magazines.
Then I get a Fudgsicle
and turn on *The Dating Game*.

The show is almost over
when Kate starts to cry—low and soft
and building up.
I run to her room. She's standing in her crib.
She sees me and stops crying
but looks dazed.
Then she wails and grabs the railing of her crib.

"Mama mama mama!"

"It's okay, Baby Cake. Remember me? I'm Mimi.

We blew bubbles together," I say,

wishing I'd brought bubbles tonight.

"Can I pick you up?"

She shakes her head and cries more.

"I'll be right back," I say,

and bring a bottle from the fridge.

But she throws it to the floor.

"Mama mama mama," she cries louder.

"Kate, you'll wake up the neighbors,"

I say, even though it's only eight o'clock.

I help her lie down again, but she stiffens

and pops up, pulls on the crib railing.

So I take her out of the crib

and carry her to the living room.

She wants to get down

and cries more.

Now I don't feel like babysitting.

I'm no good at it,

and I want to cry, too.

I try holding her and feeding her

and rocking her and putting her back in her crib,

but she cries all through *My Three Sons*.
I can't take anymore,
so I call the number by the phone.
It rings and rings, but no one answers,
and I drop the phone back into the cradle
and look at the clock. Maybe they'll be home
in an hour, or two hours. Or three.

I'm thirteen now and should be able to handle
things like this on my own, but I can't handle this,
and I call home.
When Mama answers, I can only talk
between Kate's screams and my sobs.
I feel like I'm drowning, but when Mama says,
"I'll come soon, Mimi-chan,"
I know I've found a rowboat to roll into
and rest.

When Mama comes, she picks up Baby Cake
and coos to her. "What a good girl you are.
Why are you crying for Mimi?"
Mama takes her back to her room
and changes her diaper.
"Where's her bottle?" Mama asks,
smoothing Baby Cake's soft hair

as she drinks,

watching Mama. And blinks.

"She's tired. That's all," Mama says,

and picks her up, sways in place.

Kate's eyes close and she looks heavy on Mama's
shoulder.

I take the bottle from her limp hand.

Mama lays her gently in her crib.

Baby Cake sleeps on,

and Mama waits with me in the living room,

watching *Hogan's Heroes* until we're sure

Kate will stay asleep.

"I'll go now," Mama says. "You'll be fine."

I know why Mama is leaving

instead of staying with me—

so Kate's mom and dad will see

that everything went fine

while I was in charge.

Going Home

When Papa's older sister, Fiona,
was fourteen, she was burned in a fire.
But she survived,
and after that, they called her Phoenix—
the bird that rose from ashes.
Auntie Phoenix was the only person in Papa's family
who kept in touch with him
after he and Mama got married.

Today, Auntie's husband called.
Last night she had a heart attack
and died
in peace.

Papa's leaving for her funeral in Baltimore.
I'm not going

because I need to keep Mama company.
Mama's not going
because she has to stay with me.
And because when Papa married Mama,
his family disowned him.

Jitter Legs

Jitter legs is not a dance
or a disease
or the feeling you get when you walk too long in the
snow.

Because Papa is still in Baltimore,
he can't drive me to school today—
my first day of eighth grade.
But he and Mama had already decided
I'm old enough now to take the school bus.
And I have decided I'm old enough
to walk by myself
to the bus stop at the end of the road.

Timothy had said that on our first day of school
he'd meet me down the street from Mr. Dell's.
But he isn't here,

so I keep walking
and tell myself, "Everything will be okay.
It's only school,
this year I'm one of the big kids,
and I'm not new.

Timothy is not at the bus stop,
and neither is the bus.
A few cars, a motorcycle, and
a truck carrying chickens whiz by me
on the road into town.

The little fear comes back, inching
from my chest to my arms
and legs, up to my head.
It's hard to breathe.
Who will my teachers be?
Will the kids act differently this year
around me, toward me?
Will I make more friends?
Will Timothy come on time?

I can't just stand here and wait,
so I walk in a circle, taking big steps

like the astronauts on the moon.
They must have been more afraid
than I am now, but they
walked around the moon anyway,
and did what they had to do.

Finally, Timothy comes down the hill.
"Sorry I'm late," he says, and hands me a Pop-Tart
that's still warm.
I stop walking, relieved to see him, and take a bite.
Then the bus rolls down the road
and thuds to a stop right in front of us.
The door folds open.
Timothy waits behind me.

Jitter legs
is standing at the bus stop,
scared that eighth grade will be just like seventh,
but knowing you have to get on the bus
and do what you have to do.

One Small Step

Loneliness is
> Watching your sea-blue home floating in the
>> blackness
> hundreds of thousands of miles away.

> Leaving your cousins
> to live where no one speaks your language.

> Being abandoned by your family,
> then visiting your favorite sister after she has died.

> Waiting at the bus stop by yourself
> and feeling like it's last year all over again.

Fear is
> Standing on the ladder of Eagle
> before taking one small step—

one giant leap—
into the ancient dust.

Lining up on a gangplank in Los Angeles
before taking your first step
into your new country, *Amerika*,
with your new husband,
knowing you can never go back home.

Gathering with thousands of other people
about to step together
to a song of freedom and equality for everyone,
no matter what it may cost.

Watching the bus door open
and reading WATCH YOUR STEP
as you lift your foot
on your first day of eighth grade.

But courage is
Taking that one small step
anyway.

Eighth Grade

The not-so-good things about eighth grade:
 The bus route home takes so long that I almost
  get carsick
 Miss Bonne said I'm flabby
 There's a lot more homework in eighth grade
 No one looks like me, but a new boy comes close
 Kids think I should have a crush on the new boy
 Girls still can't take shop

And the things that are pretty great:
 I have Mrs. Stanton again for science
 We're studying the space program
 I like cooking better than sewing
 I eat lunch with Stacey and Timothy
 Miss Bonne thinks I should try out for volleyball
 The hills are beginning to look like giant bowls of
  Trix

New Boy

A new boy
has started eighth grade—
Victor.
He's in the class with all the geniuses.

Victor is taller than most of the boys,
but that's not the only reason he stands out.

He carries a stack of books under his arm,
instead of taking only the ones he needs
from his locker between classes.

Victor sits by himself at lunch,
reading.
Every few minutes he brings his sandwich to his
mouth
and takes a bite,

then puts the sandwich back on the wax paper
without taking his eyes off his book.

I know he eats alone because
he's new
or shy
or the only boy in school
with an Afro.

We're Having Mr. Pease for Lunch

Our home ec class is going to make lunch
for a teacher. First
we have to decide who to invite
and what to make.

"Let's ask Mr. Pease," Karen says.
"He's not married and doesn't have anyone
to cook for him."

Everyone thinks that's a good idea,
and Miss Whittaker's face turns rosy.
Stacey volunteers to give him the invitation
because she has pretty penmanship
and fancy stationery.

Miss Whittaker says we should plan a balanced
menu
    and make simple dishes that we can prepare ahead,

so on the day of the lunch
we'll just heat them up and arrange them nicely.

She writes three headings on the blackboard:

Appetizer or Salad   Main Course   Dessert

We call out our ideas,
wearing our aprons that we sewed last spring
and our hairnets.

Potato Salad	*Meat loaf*	*Chocolate cake*
Salad	*Spaghetti*	*Banana splits*
Potato chips	*Macaroni*	*Rice pudding*
	and cheese	
	Ham sandwiches	
	Barbecue ribs	
	Tuna casserole	
	Roast lamb	
	Pork chops	
	Roast chicken	
	Beefaroni	

Miss Whittaker steps back
and studies the blackboard,

twirling a strand of her hair.
"I have an idea—what about . . ."

Salad with iceberg　　*Oyster stew*　　*Pudding parfaits*
　　lettuce and
　　tomatoes
Corn bread

Everyone thinks Miss Whittaker's menu is a good
idea.

"We have four kitchens and sixteen girls," she says.
"Each kitchen will make one item,
and one girl in each group will
plan the ingredients and the shopping
and supervise the cooking."

I've never heard of oyster stew or pudding parfaits,
so I can't make them
(but I will taste them),
and a salad with only three ingredients
is too easy.

"My kitchen can make the corn bread," I say.
"I make it all the time at home."

"Then you will supervise," Miss Whittaker says,
touching the chalk to her chin. "Thank you, Mimi."
The other girls in my kitchen—Karen, Joyce, and
Debbie—
say *okay, fine, sure.* It's hard to tell if they're happy
because we're making corn bread
or because they're not in charge.

How to Make Corn Bread

This is how we make corn bread,
Papa style:

Assemble your ingredients:
    cornmeal
    sugar
    eggs
    milk
    baking powder
    baking soda
    salt
    buttermilk
    flour
    butter

Buttermilk?

Preheat your oven.

What are we doing with a frying pan?

Put the skillet in the oven.

In the oven? Are you sure?
Why?

This is how we make corn bread.
Now, mix all the dry ingredients
in one bowl.
And all the wet ingredients
in another.

What are we doing with the frying pan?

It's for the corn bread.
You'll see.

But we make corn bread in a brownie
pan.
Where's the brownie pan?
Are you sure we're making corn bread?

Then fold the wet ingredients
into the dry,
but don't stir it too much.

It's all lumpy.

That's okay. It's supposed to be.
This is how we make corn bread.

Is this Japanese corn bread?

Now, take the skillet out of the oven—
use the pot holders or you'll burn your hands.
Put some butter in the skillet
and swirl it around.

It sizzles, like when you toss
snow
at the woodstove.

Then, put the batter in the skillet.
Put the skillet back in the oven.

Where's the brownie pan?
I don't think we're using one.
She's using a frying pan.
That's weird.

Bake it thirty minutes, until
the top is golden.

I'm not eating this.
It's not real corn bread.

This is how we make corn bread.

It comes out of the oven like
warm crunchy softness.

You should taste this corn bread.
It's really good!

Victor

I stop at Victor's table at lunch.
He's eating an egg salad sandwich
and reading *The Autobiography of Malcolm X*.

He looks up at me,
chewing.

"Hi, Victor," I say. "Do you want to sit with us?"
I turn to where Stacey's sitting
so Victor can see who *we* are.

"Oh," he says,
and shrugs. "Thanks."
He looks at his book
but doesn't close it.

I look at Stacey and shrug.

She shrugs back.

Then I say to Victor,

"Well, we want to tell you . . .

you should carry only the books you need

and keep the rest in your locker."

I want him to look up

so he can see my smile,

and know I'm only trying to help.

Crush

A few days later, Stacey and Timothy and I
put our trays at the table next to Victor's.
He turns his chair to us
but keeps his book open.

"We don't bite," Stacey says.
Victor chews his sandwich. Today it's cheese and ham.
"Where are you from?" I ask,
taking the lid off my *obentō*
slowly. No one laughs or gags,
but Timothy asks if he can have a *kappamaki*.

Victor swallows. "Rhode Island," he says,
and points to the *kappamaki*. "What's that?"
"Cucumber sushi. Take one."
I wonder why I ate so many cafeteria lunches last year

when I could have eaten this yummy food instead.
And maybe if I'd shared it,
I could have made more friends.

"You must be here because of the college," Stacey says.
Victor picks out a piece of sushi.
"My father works in the admissions office," he says,
and pops the sushi in his mouth.

The bell rings, and lunch is over.
We say good-bye to Timothy,
and Stacey says, "See you later?" to Victor.
He nods. "Later."
"He's so *cool*," Stacey says in my ear as we walk to
history.

In class, Debbie whisper-sings, "Mimi and Victor
sitting in the tree . . ."
I give her a Mifune look. She doesn't understand
that the girl who wants to *k-i-s-s* Victor
is not me.

Fall
1969

Sit-in

Stacey and I are on our way to study hall
when Timothy passes us in the hall
on his way to shop.
"What are you making?" I ask.
"A table. Wanna see?"
Then Stacey says, "Be careful, Timothy—
this girl gets crazy ideas."
I look cross-eyed at her and say,
"There's nothing to miss in study hall,"
and go the opposite way with Timothy.

The shop classroom smells so good—
like sawdust and oil and hot wood
and boys. It reminds me
of working with Timothy last spring.
I feel like I belong in this room,
and sit at one of the tables.

The boys at the table look at me
but don't say anything.

Mr. Sperangio comes in.
I must stick out, because he sees me right away.
"I believe you're in the wrong class.
This is shop."

                    "I know. I want to be here."

The boys laugh.

"Look here, young lady," he says,
"you can't do that."

                    "But I know how to use all the tools,
                    so you won't have to train me."
"That's not the point."

The boys stare and twist and laugh
and look at Mr. Sperangio
to see what he'll do next.

"You need to go back to study hall."

                    I put on my best smile, and
                    say, "But I'll learn more here
                    than in study hall."

The boys say, "Oooh."

"This is not a conversation,
Miss Oliver. Either go to study hall
or the office. It's your choice.
But you can't stay here."
                    "What difference would it make
                    if I sat here and listened?"
"Do you want detention,
young lady?
Because that's what you're asking for."
                    I don't want detention again.
                    I do want to take shop.
                    So I get off the stool.
"That's a wise decision," says Mr. Sperangio.

At lunch, Stacey says, "You were late for study hall."
And I tell her about shop.
She says, "I love drama. I'll go with you next time."
That's another thing I love about Stacey—
she knows there will be a next time.

Civil Disobedience

Stacey and I hook our pinkies outside shop.
"Ready?" I ask.
We know what will probably happen
if we go in. "Yeah," she says,
and we stroll into the class.

The boys watch us.
Mr. Sperangio watches us.
Stacey and I sit at different tables.
Silence
and then Mr. Sperangio's footsteps
squeak toward me.

"Young lady,
I thought we already settled this."

I glance at Stacey,
then say to him, "I just want to sit
    in your class.
I want to take shop."
"So do I," Stacey says from across
    the room.

"This is getting interesting," says a boy at my table,
and leans forward on his arms
to watch what happens next.

Mr. Sperangio puts his hands on his hips
and frowns, his face growing pink.
"This isn't going to happen
in my classroom. You girls are in defiance of the rules
and need to be disciplined.
Either go back to study hall or go to the office.

             Stacey and I look at each other
             and stay on our stools.

Mr. Sperangio huffs.
"Well, ladies, you've made your decision,

so come with me to the office."
But when Stacey and I hop down
from our stools, he looks surprised.
"Well," he says,
"you're sure about this?"

                  "We're sure."
"Okay then, let's go," he says,
and we follow him to the door.

As we leave, Andrew Dutton asks,
"Why can't they stay?"
and then I think we might have a chance
of taking shop.

The Principal's Office

Mr. MacDougall presses his fingertips together
like a daddy longlegs on a mirror.

Stacey and I
and Mrs. LaVoie and Papa
are in the principal's office. My heart is pounding,
and Stacey is breathing fast,
and I'm wondering if it was a good idea
to defy Mr. Sperangio
even though we were always respectful.
But it's too late now—
we can only go forward.

"How could you do such a thing?" Stacey's mother
asks.
"Mimi, I thought you were a nice girl."

"She is a nice girl, Mother," Stacey says.

Then Papa says, "They were exercising their civil right
to protest."

"Protest what?" Mr. MacDougall asks.

Then I say in a voice as clear as I can make it,
"We think girls should be allowed to take shop,
and we want to speak up about it."

Mr. MacDougall's fingers do push-ups faster,
and then he sits forward.

"First of all, that's silly. Secondly,
there are other ways of changing what you don't like.
You take it to the school board."

"But you have to say it's okay first, don't you,
Mr. MacDougall?" I ask.

"That's right. I do. And third,
what if no other girls want to take shop?"

"No one has to do anything,
sir," Stacey says. "But the boys could take home ec
if they want."

"She wasn't raised this way," her mom says,
and looks at Papa,

who says, "I don't understand what the girls did
wrong."

"They defied a teacher," Mr. MacDougall says,
"and the rules," looking down at his desk.
"We can't have students defying authority.
It sets a bad example."
Then he looks at Stacey and me.
"You two will be suspended from school for two
weeks."
He looks at Mrs. LaVoie, who has gone pale,
and then at Papa,
who says, "Isn't that a bit harsh? Certainly,
there are other ways to handle this."

"That is my decision," Mr. MacDougall says.
"It will give the girls time to reflect
on what they've done
and how to behave differently."

I knew we could be suspended,
but I didn't think we would. And now
Stacey bursts out crying,
but Mr. MacDougall talks over her.
"Besides, what boy wants to take home ec?"

Suspended

Staying home isn't so bad.
Timothy brings my schoolwork every night,
and Papa takes it back to school the next morning,
all done.
I haven't talked to Stacey in three days,
ever since we got suspended.
I miss her, and I hope she misses me.
I hope she forgives me
for getting her in trouble.

Tonight, Timothy comes when I'm washing the
dishes.
He says, "Miss Whittaker said you can make three
balanced meals
at home—but no pizza or hot dogs. Then
you'll be caught up, except for some quizzes
that you can take when you go back."

Then he picks up the dishcloth and washes a plate.
"Did you know there's a system for doing this?"
he says, and hands me the plate to rinse.
"No—how does it go?"
"You wash the glasses first,
then the silverware, then the plates.
You do all the pots last."
"Did your uncle teach you that?" I ask.
"I heard Miss Whittaker tell your class.
It was like discovering a secret new world."
"So that's what I'm missing," I say. "But
what if you have a dishwasher?"
"You mean, like . . . yours?"
We both look at the cinnamon-colored machine
that Mama never uses
and laugh.
"Mama likes to wash dishes by hand
so she can think."

We finish the dishes without talking.
"What's wrong?" he asks.
I put the dishpan under the sink
and hang the dishcloth on the cupboard door,

and then ask, "Do you think what Stacey and I did
was wrong?"

"Wrong? You're kidding,
right? Mimi, it was the coolest thing
anyone ever did.
And brave.
What you did made me feel like I
can do anything."

What he says makes me happy.
"I'm not sorry I did it,
but I am sorry that Stacey did.
It's my fault she's been suspended.
Her mom didn't raise her like that."

"Stacey's smart
and she can make up her own mind.
But . . ."
Now Timothy's thinking,
and I ask "What's wrong?" with a little push.

"Nothing. I gotta go."
And two seconds later
he's gone.

Fine

Timothy knocks on the door
the next night, later than usual.
"Homework," he says,
handing me my books.
Then he pulls an envelope from his back pocket.
"And letter."
I would recognize that stationery
and pretty handwriting anywhere.
"From Stacey?"
Timothy nods.
"Where did you see her?"
"I took her homework to her today."

"So, you told her
what I said yesterday?"

"Don't worry—I didn't have to.
She told me to wait while she wrote this."

I tear open the envelope
and read:

> *Dear Mimi,*
> *How are you? I am fine,*
> *and I like having another vacation.*
> *I miss you,*
> *but we'll see each other again soon.*
>
> *I'm glad we went to shop*
> *and I'm glad we didn't back down*
> *to Mr. Sperangium*
> *(oops, did I write that?).*
> *And I would do it all over again.*
> *Pinkie promise??*
>
> *Love,*
> *Stacey*

"Thank you, Timothy.
That was nice of you."

"She's your friend," he says,
and I say, "So are you."

Bad News

It's not a baking day,
but Timothy is rapping on the back door
like he's late for his lesson.
Papa pulls it open and Timothy tumbles in,
face flushed—but not because he's embarrassed or
cold
or happy. His eyes are red, too.
He falls into Papa
and hangs on, shuddering.
"My b-bro-ther."
"Wesley?" I ask.
Timothy nods violently on Papa's shoulder.
"What about Wesley, son?" Papa asks,
eases Timothy away
gently
and bends to him to see his face.

"He's m-missing. His s-squad was att-k'd."
Timothy gulps a breath. "May-be   he's   d-dead,"
he sobs, and plunges his head into Papa's shoulder.

I go to him and smooth his hair
like he's Baby Cake trying to fall asleep,
and Papa pats his back
until Timothy breaks away and runs his hand under
his nose.
I hand him a napkin.

"How did you hear?" Papa asks.
"My mom (*gulp, gulp*) called.
She's coming to get me.
I have to go back with her."

"Oh," I say,
but my heart feels so much more
                    for Timothy,
                         for Wesley,
                              for their mom,
and me.
"For how long?"

Timothy shakes his head. "I don't know,"
and then I feel bad for asking.
How could he know?

Now we hear Mr. Dell outside. "Timothy!"
"Do you want me to go with you?" Papa asks.
Timothy blows his nose again and shakes his head,
and I open the door.
Maybe I won't see him again for a long time
or forever.
Papa squeezes his shoulder and says to call us
for anything he needs—
and to tell his uncle the same thing.
I wish Mama was here, because she'd give him food
for the trip.

"Timothy!" his uncle calls. The growl
is gone from his voice, and all I hear is worry.
The turkeys gobble in the coop like a laugh track
but nothing is funny.
"Coming," Timothy says,
and turns to me. "If we don't leave till tomorrow,
meet me outside tonight?"

I feel like crying as I nod yes. It will be the
Full Hunter's Moon.

Timothy closes the door and walks across our yard
to Mr. Dell, who's standing on his side of the fence.
I watch him
watching Timothy come closer and stop.
Their bodies tell the story—
Timothy's hands answer a phone call,
Mr. Dell grows still, then folds his arms over his chest
and shakes his head.
Timothy drops his arms.

                —I press my nose to the door—

Mr. Dell looks at our house,
then at the fence between him and Timothy,
and steps over it   to his nephew.
He rests his hand on the back of Timothy's neck
gently
and guides him back to their house.

The Way We Say Good-bye: One

When Mama and I left Berkeley,
Auntie Sachi and Uncle Kiyoshi and Shelley and Sharon
walked us to the taxi parked at the curb
and helped the driver put our suitcases in the trunk
and opened the doors for us
and closed them after we settled in our seats
and stood nearby.

The taxi driver checked his map
and fixed his mirrors
and called in to say he was taking us to the bus station.
All that time, our family waited on the sidewalk,
waving and bowing, and Shelley and Sharon and I
made pig faces at one another.
They stood at the curb when the taxi pulled away,
and they were still at the curb when we turned the
corner,
out of sight.

The Way We Say Good-bye: Two

Tonight, Timothy and I meet at the fence,
but he can only stay a few minutes
because his mom wants to go home right away
in case someone tries to call her
with more news about Wesley.

I don't know what more to say, except
       Take care,

             Have a safe trip,

                    I hope everything's okay,
but I don't say them yet
because they're good-bye words,
and I'm not ready for that.

Far away, an animal howls in the night,
sounding hungry or lonely. I shiver.
"My uncle thinks it's a coyote," Timothy says,
"so be careful."

He looks up at the moon
hanging like a ripe grapefruit,
and sniffles. "I don't want to go.
I'm afraid
of what we'll find out.
But I have to go."
What can I say to my friend to make him feel better?

A ghost of light grows in the fog
as Mama opens the back door.
She's holding a box. "Mimi, come please."
"Don't go away yet," I say to Timothy,
and run to Mama.
The box is cold all over,
and I smell roast chicken and potato salad
and chocolate cake.
"For Timothy and his mother," she says.
"I'll give it to him," I say.
"You need a jacket tonight," Mama says,
and shuts the door.

When I give the box to Timothy,
he sets it on the ground
and steps over the fence,

walks to our back door,
and knocks lightly
because Mama's on the other side.

"Thank you, Mrs. Oliver," he says.
But thank you wasn't enough, because then
he says, *"Arigatō gozaimasu,"* and bows.
Mama bows back. "No . . . no.
The person who is kind to our daughter
is the one we love," she says.
Timothy's hands twitch, like he wants to hug Mama,
but she takes care of that by hugging him first,
quickly. "You be a good boy for your mother, okay?"
He nods, and sneaks me a glance that makes me
giggle inside.
But when we go back to the fence, it's not as funny.

"I'll write to you," he says.
"I know," I say. "I'll look at the moon,
and you look at the moon.
And wherever Wesley is,
he can look at the moon, too."
"Yeah, it will be like
we're all looking through the same hole in your
moon box."

He remembers.

Then it's our turn to hug good-bye,
not too quick—but just long enough
to say what we don't have words for
 I'll miss you,
  I hope Wesley's okay,
   I hope I can see you again,
    Maybe things will go back
    to the way they are now,
     Or maybe that time is over.

"You be a good boy, okay?" I say.
He smiles. "You, too—
but a *girl*,"
and we laugh.

Then he picks up the box and crosses his yard.
I wait by the fence and watch him.
I'm still at the fence when he goes into the house,
out of sight.

Reformed

Maybe
Mr. MacDougall was right—
that sitting in shop
and thinking Stacey and I could change the world
was silly.
I miss Timothy
and wanting to take shop
seems silly and small
compared to his sadness.

Maybe
I should forget
all about what I want,
and do
what other people want me to do.

Probably
when I go back to school tomorrow,
I'll tell Mr. MacDougall I've reformed.
It's the thing he wants me to do,
but

Maybe
it's not the right thing.

Switched

Something's going on today
at school,
like a party or a special visitor—
the president or maybe an astronaut.

In the halls
girls are whispering at their lockers,
and boys are looking at the floor
more than usual.

I put my books in my locker
because I won't need any for first period,
home ec. This might be a good time
to go to Mr. MacDougall's office
and tell him I've reformed.

"Hi, Mimi," someone says. It's Victor. "You're back."
Then lots of kids stop and say "Hi"
and "Wow, you're back" and "Nice vacation, huh?"
and even "We missed you."
Then they look at one another
like they know about the party
or the astronaut.

The air in homeroom prickles with energy,
like right before a thunderstorm.
But Mr. Wall takes attendance as usual
and as usual Mr. MacDougall makes announcements
over the loudspeaker.

Finally, the bell rings
and I walk to home ec.
I'll need to show Miss Whittaker
the list of balanced meals I made at home.
But when I get to the classroom,
something's different—
I've gone to the wrong room!
and step back,
look down the corridor. No,

this is the right room.

But, it's filled with boys.

Andrew, sitting closest to the door,

waves wildly for me to

go to . . .

"Shop?" I ask.

"Yes!" he mouths.

I walk as fast as the rules allow

to shop,

and see a room full of girls.

And Mr. Sperangio with his hands on his hips.

"Look here, young ladies," he's saying to them. "You
can't be here.

And what did you do with the boys?"

When I walk in, and he says,

"This is all your idea, isn't it, Miss Oliver?"

Karen says, "No, it's not. She was on suspension,
remember?

And that was all your idea."

I can't believe what's happening,

but Karen pats the empty stool beside her

and I sit.

"You'll all go to where you belong
or to the office," Mr. Sperangio says.
"Let's go to the office," Debbie says. "The boys
are probably already there."

Promises

In the office, Mr. MacDougall does his finger push-ups
and stares at us. There are thirty-three kids in the
room
and he opens the windows
so we can breathe.

He doesn't say we'll be suspended
for being silly or defiant. But he does say,
"Do you honestly think you can change the rules,
change the world,
by switching classes?"
Andrew says, "We didn't think it was fair
to punish Mimi and Stacey for trying."

Mr. MacDougall stares some more
and lifts some papers on his desk,

as if a script for his next lines is under them.
He says, "If you go back to your classes—
where you're supposed to be—
I promise to think about this.
Agreed?"

We all look at one another,
and yesses grow slowly in the room.
Then the boys go to shop,
and the girls go to home ec.
Mr. MacDougall said he would think about it—
he promised.

Where's Pattress?

Pattress has adopted the turkeys.
Every day she has sat by the fence, guarding them
until she's called into her house.

But when I go out today to feed the turkeys,
Pattress isn't at her post.
And when I feed the turkeys,
one is missing. I count them,
and still one is missing. Rufus,
the little one, is gone,
and a clump of feathers lies
behind the coop.
I run to the house
screaming, "Mama, something got the turkeys!"

Mama runs out with me, pulling on her sweater,
and I think a horrible thought:
Did it get Pattress, too?

"We have to find her . . . them. Quick!" I say,
and we go in different directions—
Mama looks around and inside the coop,
I circle the house
and then zigzag the backyard,
checking Mr. Dell's yard, too.
But we don't find Rufus or Pattress.

"I'm going to the woods," I call to Mama.
She catches up with me,
and we run, calling "Pattress! Pattress!
Where are you, girl?"
All I want
is to see her running and leaping and barking.
"Pattress," Mama calls, then puts her finger to her lips
for quiet. We listen,
and hear a low howl sift through the trees.
"Pattress!" I call, running toward the sound.
It gets louder.
Mama and I keep calling

as we run through the woods
toward it.

We find Pattress—
she's lying near a tree
on her side. She lifts her head when we come near
and whimpers.
Feathers surround her,
and I know Rufus is dead.
But Pattress is alive
and when I touch her, she nuzzles my hand
and tries to lick it.
Blood oozes from her torn ear
and ragged scratches on her side.

"Get Mr. Dell," Mama says. "I'll stay here."
But I ask, "Can you?" I don't want to talk to him.
"I—can't, Mimi. You know him better."

I don't like Mr. Dell,
and I don't care if he doesn't like me.
But I love Pattress, so
I pat her head. "You'll be okay, girl," I say,
afraid she won't be,

and run back out of the woods
to Mr. Dell's steps.
"Everything will be okay," I tell myself,
afraid I won't be.

Wheels

I step up to the back door
and bang on it,
and bang
again,
but no one answers.

What if he's not home?
  What if he doesn't want to answer the door?
    What if he tells me to go on home?

Then I run to the garage
and bang on that door
and again.
Finally it slides open,
and Mr. Dell stands there, looking fierce.

I push away my fear

and say, "Pattress is hurt, she's in the woods, and she

can't walk."

"Wait here," he says gruffly.

He goes deep into the garage

and comes out pushing a wheelbarrow

with a blanket in it. "Let's go," he says.

I run back to the woods,

and he follows.

It is sad and sweet

to see how tenderly Mr. Dell touches Pattress

and talks to her. "Good girl," he says.

She whimpers back at him.

"Something got your turkey," he says. "Probably that

coyote

we've been hearing."

"And Pattress tried to get it," I say.

"She saved the rest of the turkeys," Mama says.

Mr. Dell says, "We have to get her on the blanket

and lift her. Help me,

please."

It's the first thing he's ever said to us

nicely.

Pattress's paws hang over the edges
and her head lolls. I steady her
as we wheel her slowly to the garage.
Then we slide her onto the seat in Mr. Dell's pickup
truck.
I fold the edge over her so she'll stay warm.
I want to go to the vet with Pattress
but not with Mr. Dell.

Mama and I walk home together
slowly.
She's looking at the ground
and moving her lips,
saying a prayer, I think.
I don't know who she's praying for,
but I say one for Pattress.

Words

There has been no word about Pattress,
no words from Mr. Dell,
though I've been hoping for some
news—
words like

    The vet said she'll be okay,

or

        She's injured for life,

or

        Thank you for finding her,

or even

        It's all your fault for having those turkeys.

But Mama and I heard none of them
while we searched for Rufus
and picked up what was left of him—
more feathers, a foot,

and part of his beak—
and buried him under a maple tree in the backyard.

We've heard nothing tonight
after dinner
and dishes
and homework at the kitchen table,
until

Gunshot—
the exclamation point
of a sentence with no words.
It shakes the glasses in the drainer
and rattles my chest.
Papa swings open the back door
and looks outside.

That's when we hear the words
Mr. Dell shouts from the fence.
"You won't have to worry about that coyote
getting any more of your turkeys."

Thanks to Mr. Dell, the turkeys will be safe.
But I'm still worried about Pattress,

and slip under Papa's arm.

"Is Pattress okay?" I call.

Mr. Dell shoulders his rifle.

"She'll be fine," he says,

and nods

so deeply that it could be a bow.

Pardons

Toshirō Mifune had been living in our house
since last night, when
Walter Cronkite showed President Nixon
pardoning a turkey
so it wouldn't get eaten for Thanksgiving.

Now my mama has returned, and says,
"Mimi-chan, draw a big sign—
Pardoned Turkeys—
and put it in the front yard."
Then her eyes fill with tears for Rufus.

We come up with a plan:
Anyone who wants a turkey
has to sign a paper
promising they'll keep it as a pet

and let it die in its sleep
after a good, long life.

I tell Mama, "Rufus would be happy to know
he saved all the other turkeys
from Thanksgiving dinner."
Mama wipes her eyes,
and I make the sign and type the promise
on nine pieces of paper—one for each turkey.

Pattress will be okay, and now
the turkeys are pardoned.
I run to the coop and tell them
they have something to be thankful for.

Homework

Stacey and I are doing homework together
in her bedroom. It's the first time I've been to her
house
since she invited me in May.

Her house is smaller than mine,
but they have a garden in the backyard.
In the middle sits a silver ball on a pedestal
that reflects things almost all the way around.
She calls it a gazing globe,
and when I go home tonight
I'll ask Mama if we can have one,
so we can see the moon and the stars
without looking up.

I'm propped on Stacey's big bed,
and Tinkerbell, her cat, is stretched out beside me.

Her purring sands the air.

Stacey looks up from her history book

and puts her head in her hand. "What are you

wearing to the dance?"

"Oh," I say, marking my place with my finger. "I'm

not going."

She lifts her head. "Why not? Oh . . . ," she says,

remembering what happened last spring.

"I'll stay with you the whole time. I promise, Mimi.

So, will you go?"

"Why do you want me to so bad?"

"Because dances are fun . . .

and . . ." She looks at her book.

"What?"

"Well, do you like Victor? I mean, *like* him."

"No, but you do."

She waits for me to say "That's dumb" or "That's

great."

Instead I ask, "Did you tell your mom?"

"No—never!" she says.

Then she sits next to me on the bed.

"I'm sorry, Mimi. I didn't mean it that way."

I know what way she meant,

but I don't want to talk about it with her.
She and Timothy are the only people
who don't make a big deal
or act funny around me,
and I don't want that to change.

But she talks about it anyway:
"You know Mother. I mean, look how long
it took for her to invite you over.
She never invited my Black friends back home.
I'm so sorry about that.
I don't care if Victor is Black. I don't care
if he's dorky. Actually,
I like that about him."
"That he's Black or he's dorky?" I ask,
stroking Tinkerbell. "Or maybe you like him
because your mother won't?"
She pets Tinkerbell, then says, "No, I'm sure
that's not why. He's just interesting and smart and
nice."
"And cute?"
Stacey giggles and covers her mouth. "Yeah,"
she says, and falls onto the bed.

"So, do you like me because I'm Black and Japanese?"

"Wha-at?" Her face tells me I'm so wrong. "Of course not,

Mimi. I like you because you're brave

and dorky."

And we both laugh.

"So, why do you like me?" she asks.

"Because . . . you don't care

what people think,

except when your big toe is showing."

"Oh, that!" she says, and giggles. "That was a disgrace.

And then we caught the cooties."

"Cooties are stupid."

Then Stacey rolls over and says, "I was wondering if . . .

you would pretend to be at the dance with Victor

if anyone asks."

"Do I have to hang around him

and dance with him?"

"No, I want to do that. But, like, if my mother asks."

"Okay," I say, "but I don't think you have to worry."

"There's something else . . . ," she says. "Do you think your mother

would make me a dress?"

"I'm sure she would, but you have so many cute
ones."

"Your mom makes beautiful dresses," she says.

"And I want to look beautiful. If you want,
you can wear one of mine to the dance."

"Like from Bonwit Teller?" I ask.

"From anywhere!"

Then, we forget about our homework
and talk about the dance—how we'll switch dresses
and become each other.
But we don't talk anymore about why
she wants to keep her crush on Victor a secret.

Thanksgiving

Mama wanted to keep Shirley and Bobo,
but the other seven pardoned turkeys
went to good homes before Thanksgiving Day.

On Thanksgiving morning, she packs vegetables
and mashed potatoes, a pumpkin pie,
and a cooked chicken (because it was already
roasted at the store)
in a cardboard box.
"Take this to Mr. Dell," she tells Papa.
"He is all alone."
This is how Mama will till the soil
with Mr. Dell.

"Come with me, Meems," Papa says.
I shake my head. I don't want to see Mr. Dell.

"It will be easier to carry the food
in two boxes, so I need your help."
"Well, okay," I say, "as long as I don't have to talk to
him."

We carry the boxes across the yard
and over the fence to Mr. Dell's back door,
and knock
and knock again.
Just when I'm about to say "Let's leave them here,"
the door opens
a crack
and then wider.
Mr. Dell doesn't smile,
but he doesn't shut the door.

"Emiko made dinner for you," Papa says,
and holds out his box.
Chicken-smelling steam seeps through the flaps of
my box,
and then a miracle happens—
Mr. Dell opens the storm door all the way
and takes Papa's box.
I stack mine on top.

Mr. Dell looks at us
and says, "Thank you."
"Happy Thanksgiving," Papa says.

We walk side by side
all the way home
before we look at each other
and smile.

Winter Again

Another Try

I'm getting ready for another dance with Stacey,
and it feels the same as last time.
I wish Timothy was in Hillsborough
because, even though Stacey promised to stay with me,
I'm nervous
and want to see my friend
and laugh with him
and maybe even dance together.
Would he want to dance with me?

Papa gave me another dime before I left,
but I said I wouldn't need it this time.
He put it in my hand anyway
and said, "You never know."

The dress Mama made for Stacey
is emerald-green velvet

with an empire waist and Juliet sleeves.
"You'll be the princess tonight," I tell her,
and she asks, "You think Victor will notice?"
I shrug because I don't know what boys think,
and because a little part of me doesn't want Victor to
notice,
because then I might lose a friend.

I'm wearing one of Stacey's dresses,
an A-line style made of garnet-colored silk brocade.
It shimmers in the light.
Stacey says, "You'll be the belle of the ball."
We giggle. Secretly,
I think the dress Mama made is prettier.

This time, Stacey doesn't have to help me
put on blusher and eyeliner and shiny lips
because I've been reading the *Co-ed* magazines
in the home ec room. And I'm wearing
the happy moon pendant
from Timothy
to give me courage tonight.

"You ready, girls?" her mom says in the hall. "Time to
go."

Her dad takes pictures
and says we'll knock the socks right off the boys,
and her mom gives Stacey a bracelet to wear
just for tonight.
"All parents are the same," I say,
and we giggle again
because it's true
and we're both nervous.

As her mom drives us to school,
the streetlights seem to bow
to the princess and the belle.

Winter Magic

This dance will be different, I tell myself,
because I am older and wiser than last spring.
This time, I don't swallow giggles,
and I don't expect something brand new to happen.

As soon as Stacey and I hang up our coats
and go into the gym, she begins to dance
to "Love Child," and looks around for Victor,
her eyes glittering.
"Do you see him?" she asks.
As I look,
some girls and even some guys
smile at me or wave, and I know
this dance will be different.

"Don't worry," Stacey shouts close to me
over the music, "I won't leave you,"
and just then, Victor comes behind her,

catches my eye,

and taps her shoulder.

She twirls around and looks surprised—

but who else was she expecting?

"Hi," she says shyly.

"You just get here?" he asks.

We nod because yelling hurts our throats.

The music switches to "I Heard It Through the Grapevine,"

and the three of us start wobbling

like a three-legged stool.

It only takes a minute

for the two of them to be dancing with each other

and for me to be dancing with myself.

Suddenly I'm thirsty,

and point to the refreshment table.

But on my way there, I get stopped

by kids saying hi.

And then,

Michael from my homeroom asks me,

"Wanna dance?"

No one ever asked me that before,

not even Papa or Auntie Sachi.

The band is playing "I'm a Believer,"
and I'm laughing, and Michael's laughing
because we're doing different moves
in opposite directions.
Then Stacey and Victor come over,
and we all dance together in a circle.

The song ends
and we're puffing and sweating, and
I don't know what to say to Michael
or what to do,
so I say, "Excuse me,"
and I head to the refreshment table.
Someone taps my shoulder,
and I turn to see
nobody.
Then they tap my other shoulder,
and I turn to see
Timothy.

Welcome Back

What are you doing here? and
How are you? and
What's new?
we ask each other.
I don't hear his answers because
the music is so loud and
I'm so happy to see him again.
"Let's go outside," he yells,
and when we get there, I ask, "What about Wesley?"
He nods. "He was wounded, but he'll be okay.
He'll be in the hospital for a few months."
"I'm so glad he's okay," I say.
Timothy starts to say something else, then stops
and rolls a pebble with his shoe.
So I tell him what happened
when Stacey and I came back from suspension,

how the kids switched classes, and Mr. MacDougall's
promise.

And that Stacey will be dancing with Victor for the
whole night.

As we talk, a few cars crawl into the parking lot for
their kids.

"You look really great, Mimi," he says.

I'd forgotten he's never seen me like this.

Suddenly I don't feel like myself

in Stacey's dress and wearing makeup,

so I wipe my lips with a tissue.

"I have something," he says,

digging his fingers into his pocket.

"Close your eyes and hold out your hand."

I feel something cool and round drop in my palm.

"Open," he says.

Even in the shadows of the parking-lot lights

I see it's a copper-colored coin

with two astronauts on the moon,

and written across the bottom:

JULY 20, 1969

FIRST MANNED LUNAR LANDING

"One small step," I whisper.

Then say, "This is so cool. You're lucky

to have it," and hand it back to Timothy.

But he says, "It's yours."

The Party's Over

Stacey's mom drives up
and rolls down her window. "Mimi, is Stacey with
you?"
"Um," I say, trying to think fast.
She was supposed to see me with Victor,
not Timothy. "I'll go get her."

The music in the gym has stopped
and the lights are on,
but kids are still there—all in one corner—
and chanting, "Fight! Fight!"
and girls are screaming.
I try to see what's going on,
but there are too many people in the way.

Mr. Pease and Miss Borden rush into the crowd,
easing people aside.

I follow them, and see
David Hurley sitting on Victor, punching him,
and Stacey crouching nearby, screaming at them.

Mr. Pease pulls David off Victor
and hauls him toward the boys' locker room.
Miss Borden puts her arm around Stacey
and guides her away.
No one's helping Victor,
who's trying to sit up,
so I kneel next to him. "Are you okay?"
"My glasses," he says. They're a few feet away,
and someone shoots them across the floor to me.
His nose is bleeding,
so I hand him a tissue from my pocketbook.

"What happened?" I ask.
He shakes his head, and says,
"I gotta get out of here,"
and sits up slowly.
Someone brings him a Coke.
Chatter and silence echo in the gym
as Victor and I walk across the floor
and outside.

Timothy is talking to some kids by the curb.

"You okay?" he asks.

"Where's Stacey?"

"She left with her mom."

Papa is waiting in the car.

He doesn't act surprised to see Timothy

and says we'll take him home.

Then he asks Victor if he needs a ride.

Victor says no thanks, he'll walk.

But Papa insists, and I'm glad

he doesn't ask Victor why there's blood on his shirt.

Since Never

"I was dancing with Victor,"
Stacey whispers over the phone the next day.
"Then David tapped me to dance,
but I ignored him
and danced another song with Victor.
Then Tony asked me
and I said no.
And Carl asked me on the next song,
and then David again. I kept saying no—
they were standing against the wall,
talking and staring at us—
but I didn't want to dance with anyone else."

"That's creepy. But
you did look like a princess last night,"
I say, trying to make her feel better.

She keeps telling me the story.
"When the dance was almost over
David said to Victor, 'You better let other people
have a turn,'
like it was an order—and like I was a mannequin or
something.
So then Victor said, 'Hey, she can dance
with anyone she wants.' And that's when
David grabbed my arm—"

"I wish I hadn't gone outside. I wish
I hadn't left you."

"You didn't know," she says. "Anyway,
what would you have done?"

"I would have piggybacked David
to make him stop."

"You would—for me?" she asks.

Papa would remind me about raindrops
and hammers,
but this was different, wasn't it?

So I say, "Yes."

"Thank you," she says, her voice softer. "Anyway,
Victor pushed him away,
but then David shoved Victor down
and sat on him."

　　　"That's when I came into the gym."

"Mimi, those boys were mad at us."

My heart is pounding. It's hard to hear
that this happened to my friend.
I wipe my sweaty palms on my pants.
and say, "You didn't do anything wrong.
They did."

I hear her swallow,
and then she says, "You're right, Mimi.
Since when is dancing a crime?"

Making Sushi

Mama's showing us how to make *norimaki*
sushi in home ec. "Put a seaweed on this *makisu*,"
she says, holding up the bamboo mat for rolling sushi.
"Seaweed?" Debbie asks. "Ick."
"It tastes good. You'll see.
Then, take this rice and press it on the seaweed."

Miss Whittaker studies what Mama is doing.
"Mm-hmm," she says
   every now and then, and writes each step on the
board.

Then we fill our rice with the cucumbers and carrots
and fish cake and sweetened scrambled egg
that Mama brought from home.
She also brought sliced hot dogs
for the girls who don't want fish in their sushi.

I'm so happy that my shy mom came to school
and showed the girls part of herself—
and part of me.

Miss Whittaker says we should save some sushi for
the boys,
but everyone groans
and says the boys can make their own.
Then I say, "Only if they could take home ec,"
and Debbie calls me a rebel.

"Sushi's good," Linda says. "How do you say that,
Mrs. Oliver?"
"*Oishii*," Mama says, then says it again
slowly with Linda. "*O-i-shii.*"

"Please have a seat, Mrs. Oliver," Miss Whittaker says.
I point to the empty chair at our table,
but Mama sits with Kim and Karen,
who are popping sushi into their mouths
and saying, "*Oishii!*"
But then
the worst thing happens.
Kim smiles at Mama and bows,
and says, "Thank you, *Baka-san*,"

and Karen does the same thing.

Mama's face grows pink

and her eyes wide.

She looks at me, like she's asking "*Nani?*"

I shiver,

but then she covers her mouth and laughs.

Kim and Karen look at each other,

puzzled. "Did we say it wrong?"

Mama shakes her head and asks,

"Did Mimi teach you that?"

"Yes," Karen says. "Why?"

"She will explain," Mama says. "Won't you, Mimi?"

After school I have to tell Kim and Karen

what I did and why I lied,

and apologize.

"Well, it *was* kinda mean," Kim says.

Then Karen giggles, and Kim giggles,

"But it was kinda funny, too," Karen says,

and then I don't feel so guilty.

"Your mom is really nice," Kim says. "And she's so
cute."

My mama is cute, and it makes me happy

they think so. But she's so much more.

"Maybe you could

come to my house after school someday," I say
carefully.

"Sure. We can make more sushi."

We stop at the drugstore, where we'll go in different
directions.

"See you tomorrow," I say, heading toward Papa's
building.

Karen calls, "Okay, see you . . . *Baka!*"

And we all giggle until we're out of sight.

Decisions

Someone comes into history
and hands Miss O'Connell a note.
She reads it and nods and walks toward my desk.
My pencil makes a jiggly line in my notebook.
Notes in school are never good news
unless they're from your friend.

It says:
Please send Mimi Oliver to Mr. MacDougall's office.

Mr. MacDougall tells me to have a seat
and sits on the edge of the desk,
clasps his hands in his lap
and makes the kind of smile
that can mean he has something awful to say.
Or it can be his way of tilling the soil.

"How are you doing, Mimi?

Are you feeling at home now at school,

making friends?"

"Yes, sir."

"I hear good things about you from your teachers.

You're a star student—

a real credit to your race."

I wonder

if anyone ever said that to Mr. MacDougall,

or if he has any idea

how much it hurts.

But I nod and make a little smile

because he's the principal

and I don't know why he called me to his office.

He unclasps his hands and sits in his chair.

"I told you

I was going to make a decision about . . .

that ruckus you and Miss LaVoie instigated.

That's unusual behavior in our school,

in our town."

"I know, sir," I say. "But I wanted to stand up for

what I believe in."

"Which is?"

I take a breath,

remember the picture on the wall of Papa's study,

and say, "Equal rights and protection under the law."

He leans forward. "I have to tell you, Mimi,

at first, I didn't like what you were doing.

It was rebellious

and there's too much of that going on

in our country these days.

But when I saw the other students

supporting your idea,

I thought differently.

And then I realized you were not rebellious

but courageous.

You know what that means?"

"It means being scared

but doing it

anyway."

Mr. MacDougall leans back in his chair.

"You're absolutely right. So I've been thinking

about girls doing wood and metal work

and boys doing cooking,

and I came up with a solution

that will make everyone happy. Starting in January,
we'll have two new after-school clubs—
the Carpenters Club for the girls
and the Chefs Club for the boys.
How about that?"
He smiles, wanting me to say something.

"That's great, Mr. MacDougall—
for now. But it's not the same as having classes."
"No," he says, "it's not, but we can't have classes.
So, that's what we're going to do.
It's my decision."

He might think the subject is closed
but I know it isn't, so I say,
"Maybe later we can have classes,"
and think *Drip, drip, drip.*

The bell rings, and he dismisses me.
When I stand up to leave, I say,
"Thank you, Mr. MacDougall.
You're a real credit to your race."

Best Prize

My last class before Christmas vacation
is science. We're doing an experiment
to distill wood, and the room smells like burning
leaves.

"Time to finish up, people," Mrs. Stanton says.
Linda, my lab partner, and I quickly write down our
results
and finish up.

The bell rings for the last time
of 1969, and we start to leave the room.
Mrs. Stanton says, "Mimi, please stay for a few
minutes."
Stacey and I are going to town after school
to shop for presents and eat sundaes,

so she says she'll wait at her locker.
Mrs. Stanton sits at the desk next to me.
"I wanted to talk to you about something
before we all go on vacation."
She's smiling a different smile than Mr. MacDougall's.

"You remember what happened last spring
with your science project?"
I say, "How could I forget?"
"That was unfortunate," she says,
"but I was so impressed with your project—
you went above and beyond what you needed to do
for the grade.
And I know it was a great disappointment
when your moon . . . disappeared.
Many other people were, too."
She goes to her desk, "I hope
what I have to tell you will make up for that."

Mrs. Stanton hands me an envelope,
which has my name on it.
"At the end of school last spring,
I nominated you to join a group of students
from all over the country"—

It keeps sounding better and better—
"to go to Cape Kennedy this summer
and learn about the space program."
"Me?" I ask.
She nods, and points to the envelope. "Open it."
Inside is a letter addressed to me
that says exactly what she told me.

"Thank you so much," I say, my heart fluttering. "But . . .
how much will it cost?"
Mrs. Stanton smiles and says, "It's a scholarship
program.
All expenses, including your housing and food,
and travel to and from Florida,
are paid by the scholarship."
I didn't win first prize last spring, but this is
the best prize.

Then I do what I never thought I'd do
to Mrs. Stanton. I hug her.
She laughs
and says, "I guess that means you want to go."

Shopping

"This is pretty," Stacey says, weaving her fingers
through a silk scarf draped around a mannequin.
It is blue and yellow, with irises and daffodils
and buttercups all melting together.

I bought Papa a CCR album at New Sounds,
and now we're looking for Mama's gift
in Cottle's boutique.
Mama would love this scarf,
but it costs three dollars more
than I have left of my babysitting money.

Stacey had already bought presents
for her mom and dad, but today
she bought "Leaving on a Jet Plane"
for her sister, Ava, who just came home

from college in Georgia—
because Stacey likes the song.

"You should keep the record for yourself
and get Ava something else," I say.
"You don't buy Christmas presents for yourself," she
says.
"Then I'll give it to you."
"Well, where's the surprise in that?"
"I'll think of one," I say,
and give her fifty cents.
Then I slip the record in my pocketbook.

"Do you girls need help?" asks the salesgirl,
who appeared out of nowhere.
"We're just looking at all the pretty things
in your store," Stacey says, putting on her charm.
She keeps smiling, but the girl
doesn't go away. She's looking at my pocketbook.
"Did you just take something?" she asks. "Did you
put something in there?"
"No," I say, "just a record."
"Let me see that," she says, tugging my strap.
"She said she put a record in there," Stacey says.

"We don't sell records here," says the girl.

"We know," I say, finding my voice,

and it's not respectful.

"You girls need to leave—now," she says,

and points to the door.

She follows us out,

and I say, "We'll just buy that scarf somewhere else,"

and Stacey adds, "And Mrs. Cottle will hear about this."

Outside, Stacey says, "She can't talk to you like that."

"Never mind. I'll get Mama some cold cream."

"Who gets cold cream for Christmas?"

I head toward the drugstore,

but the feeling that I want to bury myself in a deep, dark hole

for the rest of my life follows me. I can't get away from it,

no matter how fast I walk.

"She didn't know who she was talking to, Mimi," Stacey says,

catching up to me. "Mimi Oliver,

future astronaut. You should have shown her that letter."

"Can we please forget it?" I say,

though I know I can't. "Let's go to the drugstore
like we planned."

"Okay," she says, "but promise you won't buy cold
cream."

In the Mirror

Stacey and I sit at the counter
and order sundaes, even though
it's freezing outside
and I'm not in any mood to celebrate
anything.
Whenever I think about what happened,
my neck prickles. And even though
I can tell Stacey anything, I don't want her
to see how horrible I feel right now.
It's hard to smile when you're trying not to cry.

"Didn't you want to piggyback that girl?"
she asks. "I did."

"For me?" I ask,
and she says, "I sure did,"
and spins on the stool.

"Hey, Mimi," she says.

I look up, and she's staring at me in the mirror cross-eyed,

and then it's easy to smile.

By the time our sundaes come, I don't feel so bad.

"You girls done with school now?" asks the nice soda jerk.

We spoon our sundaes and nod.

"Well, happy holidays," he says. "Those are on the house."

After he walks away I say, "He balanced out the day," my sadness starting to melt.

Stacey licks the back of her spoon. "I've decided . . . there are jerks and nice people everywhere.

And you just have to hope you meet fewer jerks."

Then I say, "And try not to *be* one."

Just then, Victor walks in.

When he sees us, he sits at the other end of the counter.

"Did you know he was coming here?" I ask.

"No, and I can't talk to him

after what happened. I'm so embarrassed."
"He probably is, too. Those boys were jerks,
but Victor wasn't."
Stacey looks down. "You're right," she says quietly,
and glances at him.
Victor looks everywhere
but at her.

Then I say, "Hey, Victor, look in the mirror,"
and nudge Stacey.
At first he only glances up,
but when she crosses her eyes at him,
he smiles,
and crosses his at her.
I whisper to Stacey,
"That's the first step."

Then in the mirror, I see David.
He has been on suspension since the dance
ten days ago.
"Don't look, but look," I tell Stacey,
and point at the mirror.
Victor sees him, too, and sips his Coke
coolly, but his foot is jiggling.

David walks over to the counter

and sits two stools away from Stacey.

She eats a spoonful of ice cream.

"Hey, Stacey," David says

softly. She takes another bite.

"I'm sorry," he says.

"About what?" she asks.

"You know—the dance."

"I'm not the one to apologize to," she says,

her eyes darting to Victor.

Then she puts her spoon down and turns her stool

to him.

"I'm waiting."

David sighs and walks over to Victor,

who stands up.

Then David says something to Victor,

very low, and Victor nods

solemnly. It doesn't look like forgiveness

but it might be a step.

I've never had proof about my science project,

but I've had suspicions,

and when David comes back to Stacey,

I ask, "Where did you put my moon last spring?"
David frowns
and walks out of the drugstore.
Then Victor slides his Coke down the counter
and sits near us. "That was good," he says to me.
"But you just let him get away with it," Stacey says.
"No, I didn't—he knows I know. And that's enough,"
I say,
and finish my sundae.

Excuses

At Stacey's house, I have to relive the scarf thing all
over again
  when Stacey tells her mom.
  "I don't think that girl meant anything by it,"
  Mrs. LaVoie says. "I think you read
  too much into it."
  "Mother, you should have heard her,
  and she practically grabbed Mimi's pocketbook."
  "But who would ever think Mimi,
            of all people,
  would shoplift?"
  Maybe Stacey's mother can't imagine
  anyone thinking that way about her,
  or she doesn't want to think anyone she knows
  would shoplift.

Or she feels bad about how she acted
before she met Mama.

All at once, I understand
why Stacey keeps telling the story,
why she can't let it go,
and why her mother is making excuses for that
salesgirl:
They're embarrassed.
They've never had anyone like me or my family so
close.
And this is a whole new world for them,
with all new rules.

All at once, I'm not mad or sad
or embarrassed anymore.
Instead, I hug Stacey and then her mom
and pardon them
for their confusion
about everything, because,
just like me, they are learning
how to take
one small step.

The Exchange

Stacey's mom is driving me home.

We pass Cottle's,

which is still open.

I want that scarf for Mama,

and this will be my last chance before Christmas.

I have to try again.

"Please stop, Mrs. LaVoie," I say.

She slams on the brakes. "Goodness, Mimi—what's wrong?"

"I want to go back to Cottle's."

"Whatever for, dear?" she asks.

"My mom would really love that scarf."

"Well, if you're sure . . . ," Mrs. LaVoie says.

"I'm sure," I say,

and she parks in front of the store. They open their doors,

too, but I say, "I want to go in alone."

Stacey says, "I want to tell that girl where to go,"

and her mom says, "Don't talk like that."

That salesgirl is still here.

She rushes up to me. "I thought I told you to leave."

"I want to buy that scarf with flowers on it."

"So, you didn't find it somewhere else," she says

with her hands on her hips. "We're about to close
up,

so are you going to buy it or not?"

"I am, but . . ."

She whips the pretty scarf off the mannequin

and follows me to the register.

"Don't worry," I say. "I won't steal anything on the
way."

"Gift wrap?" she asks at the counter,

snipping off the price tag with a pair of scissors.

"Does that cost extra?" I ask.

"A dollar."

"No, thanks."

She presses the keys on the cash register

and says, "Fifteen fifty."

This is the problem,

but I'm prepared. "I only have thirteen dollars."
Her mouth stays open for a year,
then she says, "What are you trying to pull?"
"Nothing," I say. "I don't have enough money . . .
but I have this," and take the Apollo coin
that Timothy gave me out of my pocket.
"Can I pay the rest with this?"

I'm scared she's going to throw me out again,
but she takes the coin and holds it near the lamp,
turns it to see both sides. "This is a real collector's
item,"
she says, looking at me through her hair.
"Okay, it's a deal."
I try to smile.

She sets the coin on the cash register,
places tissue paper in a Cottle's box,
and lays Mama's scarf inside.
"I can't pay for the box," I say,
and she says, "It's free."
I'm glad she's not a chatty salesgirl,
because my throat aches
whenever I think that coin won't be in my pocket
anymore.

The front door opens.
She calls out, "We're closing,"
and a man says, "I need something for my niece."

She ties a bow on the box, and I turn around to
leave—

and there's Mr. Dell, taking up the whole aisle
and looking at me.
He pulls off his red-checkered hat
and holds it with both hands.
My heart is pounding out of my chest
and I have jitter legs really bad.
I have to get out of here,
but the only way is past Mr. Dell.
I take a step toward him,
and he does something surprising:
he moves aside
and says, "Pardon me."

In the car, Stacey turns around and asks, "You okay?"
I shrug. Mama will get a beautiful scarf for
Christmas.
But I just gave away something
much more precious than two dollars and fifty cents.

Expressions

Papa went to a conference in Boston three days ago
and is supposed to come back today, Christmas Eve.
But he called us at two thirty
to say he's still four hours away
because the traffic is crawling
after the snowstorm.

"Okay," Mama says,
but I know she wants him home now,
just like I do.

I hear Papa say, "I love you,"
and she answers, "Drive carefully," which means
"I love you, too."

While we wait, Mama and I write *nengajō*,
our New Year cards, which we'll mail after
Christmas.

Then she makes a pumpkin pie
and I go upstairs to wrap presents—
Papa's record, Stacey's record,
which I put in a shoebox,
and Timothy's Cheez-Its,
his favorite.
Then I refold Mama's scarf in the Cottle's box
and wrap the box in Christmas paper
and a gold bow.
And so that she never has to guess, I write on the tag:

> *Merry Christmas, Mama.*
> *I love you.*

Visitors

A car comes up the driveway
and a door slams shut.
Papa is home!
Then another door shuts
and another and another.
Then the front door bursts open
and in tumbles Papa—
and Auntie and Uncle and Shelley and Sharon!

"Surprise!" they all shout.
"Merry Christmas!"
Mama covers her mouth with her apron
and sinks to the stairs.
"Bikkurishita!" she says. "So surprised!"
Her eyes glisten as she looks at her family.
"Emiko, dear," Auntie says
and sits next to Mama,
who's shaking.

"Aren't you happy to see us?"
Mama nods hard, and says,
"I thought you were ghosts."
Auntie holds out her arm. "Feel—
I'm real." Then,
"Mimi, bring your mom a glass of water."

After Mama recovers,
they tell the story—
Uncle Kiyoshi sold the house we had lived in
and their apartment building
because he had too much to manage
and wants to travel before he dies.
Papa knew about their trip here for weeks
and kept it a secret
for Christmas.
"How long will you stay?" Mama asks.
"Until the girls have to go back to school
on January fifth."
"Then you'll have to leave on New Year, right?"
"No, Auntie," Sharon says. "We flew here."
Nobody's saying
(but we're all thinking)
that now our relatives are rich.

Gifts of the Magi

Last Christmas, we were in Berkeley
without Papa.
This year, we're all in Vermont
together.

"This is for Mama," Papa says,
waving the box with a gold bow.
I give it to her, with a
"Merry Christmas!"

"Thank you, Mimi-chan," she says,
sliding her fingernails under the seam
to save the paper.
I hold my breath while she lifts the lid
and takes out the scarf. It floats around her throat.

"So beautiful," she says.
Her smile makes up for my empty pocket.
"You must have saved up all your money
for this scarf."

"And here's one for you, Meems," Papa says,
handing me a small Cottle's box.
"Is it from you?" I ask Papa. He shakes his head,
and Mama says, "A delivery man brought it yesterday."
The tag says:

> *To Mimi*
> *From Santa*

in small printed letters.
Inside,
tissue paper . . .
more tissue paper . . .
then . . .
the Apollo coin.

My coin! But from who?
"This is so weird . . ."
I start to tell everyone about the scarf—

but stop

because Mama would return it if she knew.

I want to know who gave me back my coin,

but I also want to still believe in Santa.

Oshōgatsu—January 1, 1970

"We're going to have a real *oshōgatsu*," Mama said,
thanks to Papa and our cousins,
who brought the special food from California.

After Christmas
we cleaned the house like tornadoes,
sweeping and scrubbing and dusting
and moving
and throwing out,
so that everything would be shiny and new,
like 1970.

The *nengajō*—New Year cards—had come all week.
Mama told me to put them in the kitchen drawer
and not read them
until New Year's Day,
or we'd have bad luck.

Yesterday—the last day of 1969—

Sharon and Shelley and I helped Mama and Auntie Sachi

make black beans, sweet omelets, red-and-white fish cakes, and vegetables

for *oshōgatsu.*

We chopped and stirred and boiled and stewed,

then put our New Year food in red-and-gold trays.

This morning, I wake up

next to Shelley, who's next to Sharon.

My bed is cramped,

but we wanted to make up for a year apart.

The sun is rising through the clouds.

I tiptoe downstairs.

Mama is already awake.

She gives me an envelope, and says, *"Akemashite omedetō gozaimasu!*

Happy New Year!"

Inside is a brand-new five-dollar bill

that smells like fresh ink

and feels like a new leaf.

Then Papa comes into the kitchen
and says, "Happy New Year!"
And one by one, everyone wakes up
and says, "Happy New Year!"

Then no one says anything, and Mama
is looking like Mifune.
Papa whispers to me, "No man has come to the
house."
"Oh, that's right," I say.
She pours warm sake into a shallow cup and gives it
to Papa.
He raises the cup, in thanks for a good year, and drinks.
Then he pours some for Uncle
and then for Mama
and then for Auntie.

Shelley and Sharon and I have some, too.
When I sip, the sake prickles my throat
and warms me all the way to my forehead.
We giggle
and after one sip, we stack our cups
and ask for cocoa.

Marilyn Hilton   363

Then Mama brings the *nengajō* from the drawer,

and we open them one by one.

"Here's one from Mr. Singh," she says.

Mr. Singh shared an office with Papa at Berkeley.

"How did he know about these?"

"Word must get around," Papa says.

Then Mama picks up another card. *"Nani?"* she says,

and hands it to Papa.

He reads it, then takes off his glasses,

and says, "Excuse me," and leaves the room.

Mama shows me the card.

It's from Aunt Eleanor,

Papa's little sister,

and I think, *It's a step.*

After Mama wipes her eyes,

I ask, "If Uncle Kiyoshi comes across the threshold,

does that count for good luck?"

"No. He's family," she says,

and her brow puckers again.

But as we're cleaning the kitchen,

the doorbell rings. "I'll get it," I say.

"Maybe it's a man!"

I open the door
and can't believe who I see—
Mr. Dell.
And Timothy's standing behind him
with a face that says
"Remember this day."

Confessions

Mr. Dell pulls his checkered cap
off his head. "Are your parents home?"
"Y-yes. Come in," I say.

Papa and Mama come out to greet them.
Mama's wiping her hands on her apron.
"Happy New Year," Papa says,
and shows them into the living room.

"My uncle has something to say," Timothy says
after they sit down.
Mr. Dell lays his cap beside him
and runs his hand through his hair.
"Did you have breakfast?" Mama asks,
and Auntie comes in with a tray of coffee.
"Thank you, ma'am," Mr. Dell says,

and then, "Please stay here, Mimi."
I sit on the edge of the hassock,
so I can make a quick exit if I need to.

Mr. Dell takes a sip of coffee,
and then says, "When you pardoned those turkeys—
or when you found Pattress—
I knew I needed to say this. It has nagged me
and it won't let go."
Auntie comes in with orange juice for Timothy.

"I owe you an apology," he says.
"For what?" Papa asks,
and Mr. Dell raises his hand.
"Good neighbors are hard to come by.
I've been a terrible neighbor. I've been a terrible . . .
person."
He squeezes one fist and then the other.
"I flew missions in the war—
over Tokyo, ma'am," he says to Mama.
"I dropped bombs. It wasn't hard
if I didn't think about where they were going.
And, I'm sorry, but all these years I haven't thought
about

where they went. But then you folks moved in."
"And we reminded you," Papa says.
Mr. Dell looks away.

"So, even though I don't deserve it,
I'm asking for your pardon.
Just like for those turkeys."

Mama slips her hand up to her mouth
to cover a smile. I know what she's thinking—
that Mr. Dell isn't a turkey—
because it's what I'm thinking, too.
Instead, she says, "Don't worry, Mr. Dell.
We will all be good neighbors now."

Mr. Dell takes his cap and stands to leave.
"I just wanted you to understand,
and I hope one day you will forgive me."
Mama says, "You are pardoned."

After Mr. Dell shakes Papa's hand,
he looks at me with a little nod.
I'm not afraid of him anymore—
in fact, I like him,

because now I know what's underneath his crust.
I might never have this chance again,
so I say, "Thank you for the present."
Mr. Dell frowns like he's trying to remember
and says, "I don't know what you mean."

Then he and Timothy leave,
and Mama and Papa and I go down the walk with
them,
    saying "Watch your step" and "It's cold out here,"
    and wait until our neighbors go back home.
    Then I say, "That was weird,"
    but Mama says, "That is love."

Vermont Neighbors

I used to think the people of Vermont
were like the snow—
crusty,
chilly,
and slow to thaw.

But now I think
they're what's underneath.
Like the crocus bulbs making flowers all winter
in the dark earth—
invisible until they push through the snow—
and like the cicadas growing
underground for years—
until they burst from the ground—
the people of Vermont

do their hardest thinking
and their richest feeling
deep inside,
so no one can see.

Full House

A few hours later,

Baby Cake comes with her mom and dad.

She toddles into the house, and says,

"Omedetō," in her baby way.

Mama hands her an *omochi* ball

and then a money envelope,

which Dr. Haseda puts in her pocketbook right

away

so Kate won't eat it.

Then Timothy comes back.

"It's boring over there," he says,

and soon Stacey comes with her parents.

The adults go into the living room

to watch the Rose Parade,

and the rest of us sit at the table

and play Go Fish and Old Maid and Crazy Eights

because we can't play any card games in our house
that use money or have names like liquor.

"It's too bad there aren't any boys here,"
Sharon says, "or we could play Truth or Dare."
"Excuse me," Timothy says, sweeping his cards into
his hand.
"You're different—you're Mimi's friend," she says,
and we all laugh.

Baby Cake is sitting in my lap.
She keeps grabbing my cards,
but I'd rather play Pat-a-Cake with her
and name her toes—

       Piggy Wiggy

          Penny Rudy

             Rudy Whistle

                Mary Hossle

I grasp her big toe

        aaaannd

      —Kate wiggles and squeals—

            Big Tom Bumble!

Then I notice the TV sound is soft,
and Papa is talking very low.

All of us in the kitchen
whisper our game.
"Got a queen?" "Go fish."

"I might be heading up a new program
in the fall," Papa says. "African American studies."
"That would be a great opportunity for you,"
Dr. Haseda says.
"Yes," Papa says, and sighs. "And a lot of work.
But the administration sees a new decade ahead
with changes."
"Congratulations, man," Rick says,
to the clink of many glasses,
and Papa says, "So, we'll be staying here for a while."
And I hear more clinks.

In the kitchen Shelley says, "A toast
to your dad," and we all lift our glasses
of ginger ale and Tab and root beer.
She clinks my glass
and says, "*Omedetō gozaimasu* . . .
y'all!"

This Year and Last Year

We girls are sleeping in my room—
Shelley and Sharon and I in my bed
and Stacey in the rollaway.
Outside, the waning crescent
is just a peel of a moon.

"Do you sleep on the floor at home?" Stacey asks.
"No," Sharon says, "but we can here."
We all get out of bed
and put the mattresses on the floor.
"This is how to sleep *Nihon-teki*," Shelley says.

"What did you dream about last night?" Stacey asks.
I had told her about *hatsuyume*.
Sharon says, "I had a bad dream—
a rat was chasing me around the house

and trying to bite me."
"I hate those dreams," Stacey says. "Then
I'm so happy to wake up."

Shelley says, "Mine was a nightmare, too—
school started early and I didn't have my
homework."
"I hate those dreams," I say.

I wonder if my cousins are lying.
I wonder if they really had good dreams
but don't want to tell them—
don't want to let them go.

Then Stacey says, "I dreamed I was riding in a car
with Victor, and Mother was driving.
I wonder what that meant."
"You'll have to write and tell us," Sharon says.

"What about Mimi's dream?" she asks,
and they all turn to me.
I dreamed about flying again,
this time in a spaceship.
I will not let go of that dream,

so I say, "Hmm,
I didn't dream last night."

Then I close my eyes to the moon,
and the girls keep talking. Soon
their voices sound like snow against the windows.

    I am drifting
                 to sleep,
                 eager
                                 to fly again.

Adventure

Our cousins left this morning for the bus stop
early, as the sun painted the snow
in rose and flame.

We walked our family to the Malibu,
and after Papa got them settled in,
Mama handed Shelley a box
wrapped in a spring-colored *furoshiki*.
"You didn't have to pack us a lunch," Auntie Sachi
said.
And Mama said, "It's a long bus ride to the airport."

"Bye-bye," we said to our cousins, and waved
and bowed as Papa backed out of the driveway.
And even though Sharon and Shelley and I are a
year older,

we made pig faces
until Mama and I could see only a tail of exhaust.
It's what we'll remember until we see them again.

Now our house, with only three of us,
feels twice as big as it did at sunrise.
It's funny how people can take up so much room
in your heart
but you still have plenty left
for someone else.

Timothy knocks on the back door, his eyes wide,
and asks, "You up for an adventure?"
and Papa says, "Let's be ready in five minutes,"
like he knows a secret.

Mr. Dell is waiting out front in his truck.
Mama and Papa sit in the backseat.
"Where are we going?" I ask Timothy, beside me up
front.
"You'll see."

Full Cicada Moon

We're flying
in Mr. Dell's plane!
Timothy is sitting behind me.
And I'm sitting beside Mr. Dell—
in the copilot's seat.
Below us
lies Hillsborough,
the holiday lights,
the drugstore,
Dr. Haseda's house,
the college and Papa's office,
and a huge Peace sign shoveled in the quad.
There's the Trailways bus stop outside the diner,
my school,
Stacey's house,
and the web of roads
connecting all the places and the people in this town.

Mr. Dell banks right, turning us

away from the sunset

and toward a blueberry sky glittering with stars.

"You fly now," he says.

"Me?"

"Take the yoke," he says, and gives me a thumbs-up.

I grip it tight

to steady my shaking hands,

and we fly the plane together.

Then he returns us to the airfield.

Papa and Mama are by the hangar,

jumping and waving.

But I wave harder, my heart fluttering

with joy and peace and love.

I am

                    a daughter

                                        a neighbor

                        a friend

                                            a scientist

            a poet

                        a future astronaut.

The stars and the moon,

the sun and all the planets,

every cell, every atom,

every single snowflake

belong in this universe.

And I,

Mimi Yoshiko Oliver,

belong here, too.

This year

I reached for the stars.

One day

I'll touch the moon.

But tonight

soaring.

am

I

ACKNOWLEDGMENTS

The story of *Full Cicada Moon* came to me nearly fully written, told by Mimi Yoshiko Oliver, a sensitive, intelligent, determined, and courageous girl. If you asked Mimi who this story is written for, she'd say it's for anyone who has big dreams but is short on courage.

I wrote Mimi's story in wonder and terror and awe, not knowing if I could or should write it. But along the way, the following people gave me the special encouragement and support I needed to turn Mimi's story into a book:

Josh Adams, my agent, who with one phrase gave me the courage to keep writing this story.

Namrata Tripathi, my editor, whose enormous gift, vision, and love for story sharpened and shaped Mimi's.

Keiko Higuchi, who generously and enthusiastically read the manuscript, answered my myriad questions, and shared her stories with me. And Caroline Moore for sharing her heart.

Amy Cook, Julie Dillard, Kristen Held, Ellen Jellison,

Craig Lew, Sarah McGuire, and Hazel Mitchell—the Turbo Monkeys—and Celeste Putnam and Dene Barnett, for helping set this manuscript in the right direction at a very early stage. And Marcy Weydemuller for the editorial feedback that kept it on track.

Sarah Twiss Howe Clark, my great-grandmother, for faithfully recording the weather and temperature (along with the day's events) in her diaries for most of her life. When historical weather information wasn't available, Gramma Clark's 1969 diary was.

Randi Ring Simons, my heart-sister since our year of tea in Kyoto, for her linguistic advice and her forever friendship.

My children, Julia, Emily, and Andrew, for giving me insight into Mimi's heart by sharing theirs. And, simply for being.

My husband, Leon, for his steadfast support and his suggestions that added authenticity to Mimi's story.

And everyone whose courage isn't quite tall enough for their big dreams. Facing uncertainty and fear, but taking that first small step anyway, isn't only Mimi's story—it is everyone's.

Glossary of Japanese words in
FULL CICADA MOON

Mimi uses many Japanese words in this book, and this glossary explains what they mean. First, here are some tips about how to pronounce them.

- Give each syllable the same emphasis or accent.
- There are five basic vowel sounds in Japanese, and you pronounce them like this:

    a sounds like m<u>a</u>m<u>a</u>

    e sounds like r<u>e</u>d

    i sounds like m<u>e</u>

    o sounds like r<u>o</u>be

    u sounds like t<u>u</u>be (This sound is sometimes almost silent.)

- Some vowels have a line above them (called a macron), and you pronounce them like this:

    ā means say the a sound a little longer, like "**aah!**"

    ō means say the o sound a little longer, like "**ohh!**"

WORD LIST

"Akemashite omedetō gozaimasu." – "Happy New Year!" Or, "The new year has opened—congratulations!" You say this the first time you see someone in the new year (and not before January 1). You can also say *"Kotoshi mo yoroshiku onegaishimasu,"* which means "Please treat me this year as well as you did last year."

Amerika – America or United States of America.

"Arigatō gozaimasu." – "Thank you very much." A more polite way of saying this is *"Dōmo arigatō gozaimasu."*

baka – Foolish or silly.

"Bikkurishita!" – "I was surprised!" or "I was shocked!"

chan – An endearment added to a young child's name. *Chan* is used for girls and boys, and *kun* is used for boys.

furoshiki – A square cloth, made of silk or other fabric, that's used for wrapping packages or gifts. You lay the *furoshiki* flat and place the item on it. Next, bring two opposite corners together on top and tie them in a square knot. Then tie the other two corners.

gofukuya – A tailor who makes and sells *kimono*.

hatsuyume – The first dream of the new year. It's believed that a good *hatsuyume* will come true if you don't tell it to anyone. The best *hatsuyume* have Mount Fuji, a hawk, or an eggplant in them.

hinomaru – The Japanese national flag. It's also a food made by placing a pickled plum (*umeboshi*) in the center of a bed of white rice to look like the flag.

kappamaki — A kind of *sushi* made by rolling rice and slivered cucumber in sheets of dried seaweed (*nori*).

kimono — A garment that's wrapped around the body and fastened with various ties and an *obi* (a sash that women wear at their waists and men wear below their waists). *Kimono* are made from various kinds of fabrics, such as silk or cotton, and in various styles for different events and seasons.

kotatsu — A low table with a heater attached under the tabletop. In winter, a quilt with a hole in the middle (for the heater) is placed between the tabletop and the table's frame and draped to the floor. People sit at the *kotatsu* and stay warm and cozy.

makisu — A mat made of slender bamboo sticks that are woven with string. It's used to make rolled *sushi* (*makizushi*) and other foods.

maneki-neko — A cat figurine with one paw raised to look like it's waving or calling. It's said that *maneki-neko* bring good luck.

"Nani?" — "What?" or "Yes?"

nengajō — Greeting cards for New Year's Day. In Japan, the post office delivers all the *nengajō* on January 1, when people read and enjoy them.

Nihon-teki — Japanese-like or Japanese style. For example, clothing, furniture, or even the way a person behaves can be *Nihon-teki*. (*Nihon* means Japan.)

norimaki — A kind of *sushi* made by wrapping ingredients, such as fish or vegetables, in seasoned rice and sheets of dried seaweed (*nori*).

obāsan – Grandmother. (Grandfather is *ojiisan*.)

obentō (or **bentō**) – A meal made of small portions of different foods and served in a container with sections.

"Ohayō gozaimasu." – "Good morning." You can say this greeting until noon. In the afternoon, you say *"Konnichi wa."* In the evening, you say *"Konban wa."* And at night or bedtime, you say *"Oyasumi nasai."*

oishii – Tasty, delicious.

omiyage – A gift. It is good manners to bring an *omiyage* when you visit someone.

omochi (or **mochi**) – Rice that has been pounded until it's smooth, soft, and sticky. It's used in many kinds of foods.

oshōgatsu – The New Year holiday. In Japan, people celebrate *oshōgatsu* for three days, January 1–3. To prepare for the holiday, people clean their homes from top to bottom, inside and out, and make special foods (*osechi*) during the last few days of December.

ozōni (or **zōni**) – A special soup that's eaten during *oshōgatsu*. It's often made with *mochi*, fish cake (*kamaboko*), and vegetables.

sadō – The Japanese tea ceremony (which is also called *chadō*). It is a way of making, serving, and drinking powdered green tea (*matcha*) using special utensils.

sake – A drink made from fermented rice and often served hot in small cups or glasses. During *oshōgatsu*, many families drink *sake* from special cups, one person at a time. Gold flakes are sometimes added to that *sake* to celebrate the new year.

san – A term of respect for an adult or older child. You say it after the person's last (family) name.

sukoshi dake – Just a little.

sushi – Seasoned rice shaped in small mounds and topped with other foods (like raw or cooked fish, sweet egg omelet, or vegetables), or wrapped or rolled with other ingredients (like cucumbers, mushrooms, or fish, and dried seaweed).

tempura – Lightly battered and deep-fried vegetables and seafood

Toshirō Mifune – An actor who played roles in many movies. In Japanese, the last (family) name is said first, so his name is Mifune Toshirō.